Praise for Kira Stone's *Heart of a Lion*

Rating 5 "Oh My God!! I can't say enough about this book. ...The way she wrote how Victor loved Cody and just wanted to hold him, I just loved it. I can't say enough about this author and this story. I can't wait to read what she writes next."

~ *Nicole Harvey, Gay Erotic Reviews*

Heart of a Lion

Kira Stone

A Samhain Publishing, Ltd. publication.

Samhain Publishing, Ltd.
512 Forest Lake Drive
Warner Robins, GA 31093
www.samhainpublishing.com

Heart of a Lion
Copyright © 2008 by Kira Stone
Print ISBN: 1-59998-730-9
Digital ISBN: 1-59998-458-X

Editing by Sasha Knight
Cover by Dawn Seewer

First Samhain Publishing, Ltd. electronic publication: April 2007
First Samhain Publishing, Ltd. print publication: February 2008

Dedication

For Marti, who kept asking when this one would see the light of day.

Chapter One
~ *Hot Springs* ~

England, at the foot of the Chevoit Hills, near the Borderlands, 1446

"This was a fine idea," Curran Aurick announced to the world at large.

He arched his back until the rest of his naked body floated to the surface of the steamy water. The natural hot spring formed a bath tub big enough for ten large men, but this night Curran had it all to himself. Of course, if one of the castle functionaries ever caught him here, his good fortune would take a sharp turn for the worse.

"A member of the castle's guard must not befoul the healing waters into which His Grace's lily white bottom descends," he mocked in the nasal tone of the keep's chatelaine.

Like Luthias' arse shat daisies.

Not that he had any personal knowledge of the arse belonging to Luthias, the Fourth Duke of Otterburn. Yet. Duke Luthias hadn't been home since Curran took the post of guardsman. That in no way diminished the respect and love which blossomed in Curran's heart as he listened to the epic tales spun about His Grace's battle prowess, kind heart and lusty cock.

The great nobleman had beaten back the northern marauders time and time again. His campaigns on the border separating his beautiful duchy from the Scottish rocks prevented the butchering heathens from spilling stout English blood throughout the peaceful countryside.

As his large family lived in one of the Duke's protected villages, it was a cause Curran wholeheartedly supported. It was also one of the biggest reasons he'd left home. Curran planned to spend his life chasing adventure so his younger siblings back home never needed to run in fear from the barbarians. What better way to accomplish that than by joining the Duke's army and learning the art of making war from the man who did it best?

Unfortunately, as a member of the Duke's home guard, Curran had no opportunity to take an active role in the Duchy's defense. The only time he'd had to draw his weapon was to fend off a playful attack by a quartet of maids.

Thanks, ladies, but no thanks.

It took something stouter than a virgin's plump breasts to make his cock sit up and take notice. Given the dearth of male lovers in the area, every so often Curran became tempted to take a bite of the sweet meat the ladies offered him. The notion never lasted long, for he need only look at their powdered and perfumed bodies to have his manhood bow down in defeat.

No, his body and soul belonged to men with a warrior's heart. The heart of a lion. Rare men like Luthias.

True, the Duke was aging, but far from infirm if the stories told about him contained a grain of truth. His corded thighs were laced with battle scars. His hands were calloused from a strong grip on the hilt of his sword. No doubt the man's sex would stand as tall and proud as the Duke himself.

Curran longed to know what would please so great and worthy a man in the privacy of his bedchamber. Yet, bedding the Duke was a dream destined to remain unfulfilled. His first three wives were fragile creatures, dying in childbirth or soon thereafter according to common servant gossip. The fact that he kept filling the Duchess' role even after procuring a male heir spoke to his preference for feminine charms.

Did the Duke require his wife to pleasure him with her mouth first? Or was it her warm, wet channel that His Grace preferred? Would there be anything Curran could do to entice the man to sample what pleasures could be found in the arms—and snug hole—of another man?

Curran let his thoughts linger on the arousing topic, generating an internal heat equal to the temperature of the mineral-laden water surrounding him. His engorged shaft bobbed against his flat stomach as he imagined being impaled by the Duke's cock. Soon his sex swelled with the need for release, even if it had to come from his own hand.

Under the water, his feet sought solid ground upon which to rest. The irregularly shaped wall of the pool provided an alcove which cupped his body perfectly. His fist encompassed his cock, stroking the hard shaft in a steady rhythm. He didn't have much room to widen his stance, but he did what he could with his other hand to bring his balls equal pleasure.

"More, faster," he moaned encouragingly to the Duke of his erotic dreams.

His imaginary lover complied, taking care to rub a thumb over the head of his cock on the upstroke, just as Curran preferred.

Sharp edges of the natural formation had been chipped away to provide a surface that might abrade but not slice through tender flesh. Curran relished the sensation of the rough texture against his skin as he flexed his hips.

In and out, his cock thrust through his tight fist. *No, not his, the Duke's.* And what was it Luthias was saying? Oh, yes. That Curran was a brave and honorable man. A man who pleased the Duke in so many ways...

"Yes, Yes. Take me fully into your mouth, sire," Curran said aloud. It was the last coherent phrase he could utter, for the power of his release overtook his muscles and he cried out to the full moon in one long, shuddering breath.

And in the brief silence that followed, Curran heard a shrill, avian cry which chilled him to the bone.

CSSOEO

Tanis watched from the forest as the young man soaking in the steaming pool rocked with the aftershocks of release. Moonlight cast a white glow through the mist, surrounding the man with a heavenly aura. Wet, long blond hair had been pushed back from his face so Tanis could clearly see how much enjoyment the man had wrought upon himself. He only wished he could have arrived at the beginning of the show, when he might have managed an invitation to help.

Crazy old fool, he cursed himself. He'd long ago given up on finding a male partner willing to sate his needs. Lusting after this young warrior would bring him no satisfaction.

Or would it?

Was that not a cry to "sire"? Sire, not lady? How...interesting.

Before Tanis could decide whether or not to approach the man—a stranger whose name he hadn't had reason to know before now—Athena did it for him. Her soul-rending scream pierced the night, bringing every woodland creature within hearing to full alert.

The guardsman's head snapped around as the hawk cried again. Tanis knew she was searching for him and wouldn't cease her yammering until she'd located him. Blasted bird.

But since the hawk was also his best friend, Tanis stepped out of concealment and into the ring of tall grass surrounding the pool so he could be found.

"Who goes there?" the young man demanded.

Tanis barked, his version of laughter. "A bit late to be inquiring, if you ask me. I could have had your breeches and what you put in them by now if that had been my goal."

"Tanis of Appin? Is that you?"

Tanis wasn't surprised that a member of the home guard knew of him. Most of the castle dwellers had heard of the man who brought meat to the Duke's table during these lean times. However, as he wore hunting garb and with the thick of night upon them, a human's eye couldn't pick him out against the dark trees. The man must have zeroed in on his voice, and Tanis' estimation of him rose another notch.

Athena landed on a dead branch near Tanis' shoulder. He waited until the rustling leaves quieted before he answered the guard's question. "Aye."

"Damn and blast," the other man said, slapping the water with the flat of his hand. "Do not sneak up on a body like that."

"How should I sneak up on him then?" Tanis nearly laughed again at the disconcerted look his comment had earned him.

"Best not to do it at all, not if you want to remain on friendly terms with the likes of me."

Tanis wanted to remain on friendly terms with the naked man wallowing in the hot spring. *Very* friendly terms. The problem was that he wasn't certain this man would feel the same way. Having fantasies about sex with another male didn't mean he desired the real experience, or that Tanis would fit the role of lover even if the young man did desire it. Though his face rarely caused young children to scream in fright, there were other parts of him that sometimes did. Chances were the only satisfaction he'd get out of asking this beauty for a love tussle was confirmation that he was the silly old fool he often called himself.

Yet his body refused to obey the command to walk away. His gaze was busy devouring the long expanse of a well-sculpted chest. His fingers itched to explore the curve of lower back and buttocks that hid below the spring's surface. A little insistent voice whispered inside his head that this one might be different.

While his internal debate continued, Tanis replied, "I would think you would be more alert, stealing strength from the Duke's healing waters as you are."

The guard straightened his shoulders. "There will be enough left over for His Grace when the time comes as there is little of me in need of healing."

The truth of his boast was self-evident, and Tanis rushed into speech to prevent a telling groan from escaping his lips. "What about now? Is there room for another?"

The young man seemed hesitant, and Tanis' hopes plummeted to earth like a downed pheasant. However, he was stubborn enough to enter the pool anyway, if just to take advantage of the nature-made bathtub. No doubt he could use a washing after stalking prey through wet underbrush for the last fortnight.

"Plenty, I am sure," the young man replied after a long pause. "Shall I leave you to it?"

Tanis hid his disappointed expression by bending over to unlace his boots. "I am not so wide that I require all that space to myself."

"Then you should know the company you keep. My name is Curran Aurick, a member of the Duke's home guard." This declaration being made, the young man flipped onto his belly, his large frame disappearing under the black surface giving only a quick glimpse of his finely crafted arse.

Tanis wished there was a harmless way to encourage Curran to show off the rest of his lean frame. Wide shoulders and meaty arms from his swordplay were certainly worthy of appreciation, but Tanis was more curious about what lay below the water's surface.

Tanis finished removing his boots and then went to work on his leather breeches. Athena watched him with keen curiosity until he stood in naught but a travel-stained brown tunic which hung to his knees. His semi-aroused state would be visible without it, as would the worst of the scars surrounding it. But he'd look like a damned fool if he jumped in with the fabric still on his back. The only reasonable solution that presented itself was to toss the cloth aside as he dove in.

Tanis did so, the sharp heat of the water smacking into his body. The night air had been mild for early autumn. The same could not be said for the hot spring, and he came up with an unmanly yelp.

"Hot, eh?" The guard's grin indicated that he had once tried the same trick and met with similar results.

"It was not quite so warm when I was last here."

"You come here often?"

"No." It had been he who found it, a sanctuary for animals in the area. That was before Luthias became Duke and proclaimed the healing properties of the water should be reserved for his exclusive use. Tanis couldn't explain the compulsion which urged him to seek it out this night, but he was very glad he had. "His Grace and I do not share the same taste in amusements. I find myself avoiding his presence whenever possible."

The temperature ranged from scalding to barely tolerable, depending on where he floated. The cooler area happened to be closer to Curran. He didn't want to crowd the younger man, but he didn't want to end up with blisters on his balls either. His new friend was just going to have to settle for sharing his end of the pool or abandon it altogether.

Curran shifted his weight but didn't move away. "Was your hunt successful?"

"There will be meat for the Duke's table, if that is what you are asking."

"Thank the Lord for that."

Tanis bent over with the pretense of splashing water on his face to hide his bitter expression. "His desires are important to you?"

Curran laughed, a lively, happy sound that rocked Tanis to the core. "I have yet to meet him so I cannot know his desires. My question was self-indulgent as I look forward to breaking my fast more when I know there will be meat as well as the cook's porridge to stick to my ribs."

Tanis smiled in comprehension, and then turned his attentions to removing the dirt and sweat from his body. His own rough palms did most of the work since he had no soap or clean grit to aid him. "What brings you out this night? Surely there are places to bathe within the castle walls?"

"Aye, but always under the watchful eye of a bevy of servants or men of my own rank. I prefer to have a measure of privacy when I disrobe, even if I must break a few rules to find it."

Tanis finished his chore and relaxed against the edge of the pool, his arms spread wide on the cool, dew-coated grass to prevent him from sinking. "And how do you feel about catching the rough side of the Captain's tongue when you are caught breaking the law?"

"Why worry over that when I have yet to be caught?" Curran gave him a roguish grin.

Ah, to be that young and full of himself again. Tanis reckoned he had a decade or so on the guardsman in years, but a lifetime of bitter experience had hardened him into a much older being on the inside. It soothed some of the troubled patches of his soul to see this carefree man smile with such ease.

"I bet you enjoy the skulking about as much as the privacy," Tanis said to him.

Curran nodded. "I've been trained to attack and defend inside the castle walls, but the Captain finds little reason to practice concealment. Doing so on my own is the only way to polish the skills my mentors have left out."

A bark of laughter came unbidden to Tanis' lips. The idea that men wearing metal and leather could hide among the corridors of grey stone was ludicrous. Maybe the light of the full moon had tainted the man's brains into thinking the impossible was the reverse.

"You find my attempts at concealment laughable?" There was a definite challenge in his tone.

"No, no. 'Tis not the quest to improve your skill which amuses me so much as the environs in which you choose to practice it."

Sulking a bit, Curran replied, "We cannot all be one with forest dwellers. I do all right."

"Is that an offer to demonstrate what skills you possess?"

Chapter Two
~ *A Matter of Honor* ~

Moonlight filtered through the thin clouds overhead. The glow produced enough illumination for Curran to determine that the gleam in the hunt master's eye came from desire rather than the suggestion of a contest.

Could he really be that lucky?

Though his seed had been spilled once already this night, his cock hardened anew at the possibility of pleasuring someone other than himself. Curran enjoyed the challenge of learning his partner's sexual preferences. To push his lover into release by finding that one special touch he couldn't resist. But did Tanis share his love of adventure?

Curran decided to find out. He again arched his body so that it floated to the surface, belly up. "You have only to look at me to see what I am made of," he said softly.

He heard the other man's sharp intake of breath and knew he'd assumed correctly. The question now became whether or not the hunter would act on his interest.

"Muscle and bone, same as any other man," Tanis muttered gruffly.

"Are you sure? Should you not investigate more thoroughly before you pass judgment on me?"

Curran could scarcely believe the brazen words he heard spilling out of his own mouth. Words that would surely ruin his chances of being accepted into the Duke's House as a Master at Arms if repeated in the right ears. Yet he had said them to this solitary man, betting his future that Tanis had the courage to let himself be ruled by his desire rather than his fear.

A tentative touch at Curran's brow brought the reassurance he sought. He wasn't going to be betrayed. Thank the Lord.

Curran nuzzled against the large, rough hand. "There is more of me to discover, if you wish it."

"You are no man," Tanis replied. His voice came from somewhere deep inside him, a dark and lonely place.

"What am I then?"

"A puckish sprite come to tempt me beyond all reason."

Curran smiled in the darkness. Given the position he was in—flat on his back, floating on top of the water—there was no way he could conceal his visceral reaction to the man's words. Nor did he want to. His cock pulsed against the night, ready for whatever his companion had in mind.

"I want you to touch me, hunt master."

"I must be mad."

But Tanis complied, running his calloused palm over Curran's smooth chest as steam billowed up around them, closing them off from the rest of the world. The hunter explored not only the bands of muscle ringing Curran's rib cage, but traced them to his back in a firm caress.

"Come closer," Curran encouraged him.

Tanis pulled Curran's torso against his own. From this close distance, Curran could see the dark locks curling over the tall man's shoulders. A bushy beard impeded his perusal of chin and lips and cheek. No matter. Everything he needed to see—desire and acceptance—was reflected in Tanis' brown eyes.

After several heartbeats where happy surprise deepened into sharp need, a pair of large, strong hands were under him, lifting him to the level of Tanis' mouth so that his nipple could be properly licked.

Curran shuddered at the first contact of tongue to sensitive skin. There was little difference in temperature between the hot water and the hot mouth brushing over his skin. But, oh, the difference in texture! His nipple contracted, producing a hard nub that the hunter greedily sucked. Curran wound his arm around Tanis' shoulders and clung to reflect his approval.

Tanis raised his head and glanced at Curran's thickening shaft. "I never suspected you were interested in men before I saw you here tonight."

"Nor did I."

"Perhaps both of us are better at concealment than we knew."

Curran nodded, then nipped the skin below the hunter's ear. Tanis trembled for a second, as if restraining himself from returning the gesture. At a time when those with enough coin could buy and sell pleasures of the flesh as if they were no more precious than a serving of sweetmeats, it angered Curran that he had to break through barriers forged by the same people to snatch a bit of pleasure for himself.

"I ask for everything you can freely give me this night," Curran said, knowing Tanis would hear his frustration, his anger that something so right between two men could be equally complex. "It is no less than I am willing to offer in return."

The hunt master announced his response through a shudder of his large frame. His hands tightened on Curran's ribs as if to push him away. For a second, Curran feared the man would reject him after all. That he had asked for too much, too soon.

But then the grip relaxed, shifted, and Curran found himself standing toe-to-toe with Tanis on the tiny ledge. "The next move is yours," Tanis informed him. "I vow to go no further than you."

Curran didn't hesitate. He leaned in and took the hunt master's mouth in a rough kiss. Too long denied the taste of a man, Curran couldn't marshal his need into civilized behavior. He poured his passion into Tanis' mouth, demanding that his challenge be met.

The hunt master did, pushing back with more control than Curran had, which kept their mutual hunger from spilling over into pain.

"You will be the very death of me," Tanis said when they broke for air.

"Many times over, I pray."

Curran reached beneath the water and took his own cock in hand. The hardening length approached its stoutest capacity. He brought the plump head in contact with the hunter's belly. He caressed the man's taut muscles with the tip of his cock, paying extra attention to the cleft of his bellybutton.

Because he was watching Tanis' face rather than the point of contact, Curran caught the look of surprise. The hunt master quickly doused it, and Curran wondered why. Suddenly uncertain, he pulled back. "Is it not to your liking?"

"I will be clear if your attentions offend me, warrior."

"Then why shield your enjoyment from me?"

"Sharing your body is enough to ask."

Curran thought he understood what had gone unspoken. People who rarely came into contact with others often assumed that feelings were like defective possessions. To be given sparsely, as if they were a weighty responsibility rather than a precious gift.

With time, maybe he could teach the hunter otherwise. But that would have to come later. It was not a lesson that could be learned in the space of a single sigh.

Curran continued rubbing his tall shaft against Tanis' belly as he sought more of the man's hard, hungry kisses. Since the hunter had taken on the task of keeping both their heads above water, Curran was free to use his other hand to explore.

There were ridges of scar tissue along Tanis' left shoulder. Four parallel lines, perhaps from a wolf or a large cat. An oddly shaped pattern just over his left hip indicated a wound from a puncture. Not a bladed weapon, but something that would pierce the skin and leave a hole. A broken branch perhaps, or a walking stick that had been sharpened at one end. Most troubling of all, however, was the web of knife wounds Curran discovered high and inside on both thighs.

"Stop," Tanis ordered as Curran became distracted by thoughts of what might have caused such extensive scarring. "Do not concern yourself with those."

"Are you revoking the rights you granted me?"

The hunter's eyes glittered darkly. Once or twice Curran had looked into the face of a sparring partner and known that battle lust surged in his veins, turning friend to foe in a flash of a lightning bolt. The look Tanis wore now was not dissimilar.

"One word about them, warrior, and you will not have a chance to speak of them again."

"Then perhaps I should find something better for my mouth to do," Curran replied, forcing a trickle of amusement back into his tone.

The pain endured to earn those scars weighed on Curran's mind for a total of three rapid heartbeats. Not because he ceased to care, but because after that short time Tanis suddenly released him.

Before his head submerged, Curran sucked in a lungful of air. He used the hunt master's body as a guide, following it down into the dark, steamy water. When he reached waist level, he wrapped his arms around Tanis' legs and heaved upward with as much force as he could muster. Curran came to rest on the rocky ledge where they'd started but Tanis ended up in the hottest part of the pool.

He plowed through the water and met Curran with a hard, fast kiss. "I was wrong. You are not a sprite. 'Tis the black soul of a devil that lives inside you."

Curran chuckled, which only increased the tempo of his own breathing. "I am flattered you think so highly of my tricks."

"You are fast on your feet, I grant you." Tanis tweaked Curran's nipple with his strong fingers. "I will have to teach you that being fast and bold is not always the best way to capture your prey."

Again the water provided a helping hand as Tanis lifted Curran onto the grassy bank. Curran's legs bracketed his torso. The hunter glanced at the rigid arrow of flesh rising upward, and then met Curran's eyes. "Impressive. Will it taste as good as it looks?"

"Decide for yourself." The words were supposed to be tossed off carelessly, but they had a certain desperate edge to them. Curran had a question of his own he wanted answered. Would Tanis suck his cock with the same strength and skill he'd demonstrated in his kisses?

The hunter's mouth descended in agonizingly slow increments. Curran closed his eyes, waiting for the first erotic touch.

But it didn't come...

And it didn't come...

Finally he opened his eyes, irritated at the game the hunter was playing with him. "What the hell are you waiting for?"

"I thought you were napping. I did not wish to disturb you."

Curran kicked water up with his feet. A heavy rain of droplets smacked Tanis' face. He bent forward and rubbed his whiskered cheek against Curran's thigh to wipe the wetness away. The abrasive feeling was so arousing that his cock nearly burst without further encouragement.

Gritting his teeth against the rising tide of climax, Curran growled, "Put your mouth on me, you insufferable bastard."

This time the hunter's rough laugh disturbed the night creatures. His hawk companion took to the air, landing on one of the boulders where Curran had left his clothes. She cocked her head toward her human friend, but Tanis didn't glance away from Curran's face as he lowered his lips to the twin sacs, licking and sucking the soft skin he found there.

Curran tried to press his body closer to the hunter's mouth. He pulled back and waited for Curran to resume his original position. Then that talented mouth would descend again, Curran would arch into it, and Tanis would withdraw. Over and over, neither man willing to give up, give in. Finally, frustrated beyond his ability to reason, Curran pushed too far and sent himself over the pool's edge.

"Ready to settle down, are you?" Tanis asked, after he caught Curran in his arms.

"I will not be held accountable for my actions if you delay much longer," Curran muttered. The threat was punctuated with a tongue-dueling kiss.

"Better set you up so you do not sink yourself in the process." Tanis picked out a rocky shelf near the surface and guided Curran onto it.

Once his hips rested on the small rocky ledge, Curran found two natural handholds he could use to anchor himself in place. He dug his fingers into the pliable earth and said, "Now, hunt master. I beg you."

Chapter Three
~ *Caught in the Act* ~

Tanis slid his lips over the head of the warrior's impressive cock. The young man moaned in ecstasy. Encouraged, Tanis milked Curran's member with both mouth and hand. His teeth closed over the purpled head, scraping it lightly with his teeth. He was rewarded with another long, blissful moan.

"Your mouth on me is a heavenly gift, Tanis," the guardsman told him between pants.

Tanis had never before received such a compliment. His cock throbbed with longing for this brave, foolish, caring young man. Would he lose all ground he'd gained with Curran if he asked to sample the guardsman's muscled arse?

Again, testing the waters seemed more prudent than voicing the question outright. Tanis fondled the guardsman's balls with a firm touch. His forefinger followed the seam to where it flattened against the man's body. Curran tensed, but Tanis guessed by the look on the young man's face that tension was in preparation for pleasure rather than distaste. So he kept going, applying pressure to the tiny strip of skin between the guardsman's sack and anus.

Tanis popped his mouth off the rigid shaft. "Too far?"

"Not far enough. Not nearly far enough."

Tanis softly chuckled and returned his attentions to the sweet-tasting member. Perhaps one day he would take this pup into his bed. Dawn hit his bedding through a window over his straw pallet which would give him plenty of light to explore the man's young, healthy body. Just the thought of being able to see what the water yet concealed wrung a groan from Tanis' chest.

He prodded the opening to the guard's anus, testing the fit.

"Ah," the warrior cried out.

"Pain?"

"Pleasure," Curran gasped. "I do not wish to die so quickly."

Tanis had needs of his own to consider, like feeling the young man's body quiver with release. He sucked the stiff cock harder while he plunged his finger into the opening well past the second knuckle. In and out. Up and down. A duet of motion designed to bring the most pleasure to Curran, and thus to himself.

Curran writhed under the combined assault. "Step back," he panted. "Now."

"Not even if you pressed your blade to my throat."

Tanis clung to the warrior's body as his muscles turned to stone. Curran's cock pulsed in triple time, pumping seed into Tanis' hungry mouth. The guardsman grunted repeatedly as he bucked and jerked as his seed spilled from his body. Tanis sucked every salty drop of fluid the man could spare until the warrior's hand pushed him away.

"Enough."

Not as far as Tanis was concerned, but this time he heeded the request and let the man go. He retreated to the other side of the pool where they'd started, planting his feet on the underwater shelf so he could finish himself off before Curran returned to sanity. He didn't want the warrior to feel obligated to return the favor.

"Have I behaved so poorly that you must run from me?"

Tanis raised the lids that had closed as he focused on retaining the taste of the guard's hot cock in his mouth. He found himself under scrutiny by the young warrior, and he forced himself to move his hand away from his shaft. "You need time to recover."

"Not as long as you still ache." Curran swam over to where Tanis stood. "Do you still ache for me, hunt master?"

Tanis looked down into the young man's eyes and saw no pity there. What he saw instead scared him so badly he had to avert his gaze. "Aye, though it need not be your concern."

Gently the guardsman reached out to cup Tanis' balls. That simple touch made Tanis' gut tighten with rising need.

"It is a matter of honor to me that I return some small measure of the pleasure you have given me this night if it is at all within my power to do so. Will you permit me to try?"

By the Gods, this young pup was offering him everything he wanted. Why was it so hard for him to accept it?

Gavin's face swam between them. Noble, selfish, charming Gavin. Curran was like him in many ways. Was that part of his problem? Was he linking the actions of his former lover to this young guardsman? Rejecting the act that would put Curran in charge so he didn't have to submit to another's will? Had the empty years restored none of his courage in that respect? If he had something to prove to himself, he had no right to use this warrior to do it.

"If you insist," Tanis finally said, unsure of his motives for doing so.

"I do." Curran's hand glided loosely over Tanis' eager cock. "What would please you best?"

"An end to this torture."

"With my hand?" Curran tightened his grip around the fully erect shaft. "Or with my tongue?" he suggested before licking Tanis' nipple in one long, broad stroke. "Or shall it be with my arse, which we both know is where your true desire lies?"

"I will accept your choice and be glad for it," Tanis replied through his clenched teeth. This conversation was burning away his limited patience. If Curran didn't attend to matters soon, one way or another, he'd find himself flipped over on his back, positioned so that Tanis might sheathe himself deeply between his nether cheeks and teach him not to tease a desperate animal.

"You will get nothing from me unless you tell me what it is you need."

"Damn you to hell."

"If I am the very devil as you say, I shall return there soon enough." Curran leaned in and nibbled along Tanis' throat. "Say it. Command me."

Tanis growled, a mournful note that was picked up and echoed by his avian friend. His hands gripped the guardsman's buttocks and hauled the muscular body against his own. From there it was a simple matter to slide his thick finger into the tight aperture at the base of the young man's spine.

"This is what I want, you young fool. This snug bit of flesh to part before my aching cock."

"Have at it, then."

Curran switched positions with a sense of balance Tanis had to admire. The guardsman pressed himself against the rough rock and splayed his long legs, giving Tanis complete access to the very spot he'd requested.

The young man looked over his shoulder. "My name is Curran, not Fool, young or otherwise. Get it right when you cry out, will you?"

Tanis couldn't imagine getting it wrong. His entire world had been reduced to the size of one man, Curran Aurick.

He placed his hand on the guard's bottom, parted the flesh a bit further and prepared to insert himself into that pretty, tight hole. He couldn't remember his cock ever being so large before. Suddenly he had doubts that Curran could take all of him. No matter what he'd said, he wasn't the type of man to draw pleasure from inflicting pain. "I may hurt you."

"It will hurt me far more if you stop."

Something Tanis thought long dead burst into life at that moment. A soft emotion he wouldn't name lodged in his throat making speech impossible. He responded by advancing in slow stages. A little at a time, he penetrated Curran's arse.

"Christ Almighty," the guardsman moaned.

Tanis had to agree with the sentiment. Taking the guardsman was quickly becoming a religious experience. "Can you tolerate more?"

"Press on," he grated out.

Tanis rocked forward, marveling how the young man's body adjusted to accommodate him. Soon his cock was buried to the hilt. Nothing he'd ever done before felt as pleasurable as this. "By the Gods, you were made to fit me."

"Move, man. Hard and fast," Curran encouraged him. "Take me the way we both know you want to."

Tanis didn't think he'd be able to let go to that degree. He'd spent most of his life hiding his strongest desires to avoid bringing disaster to those few willing to take him on.

Curran seemed plenty eager, but he had yet to meet the caged beast dwelling inside his heart.

Tanis did, however, pick up the pace. He settled into a rhythm that sent ripples of pleasure through his shaft and into his heart. It had been a long, long time since anyone had made him feel this good, inside and out.

"What do you take me for? An old hag? Surely you have more in you than these weak thrusts."

"'Tis the devil in you that says these things. I will not rip your arse to bloody tatters because you are too stupid to know what is good for you."

"Better to be ripped and torn than barely fucked at all," Curran replied with contempt.

Anger did what sweet reason could not. Tanis, goaded beyond his ability to resist, raided the guardsman's arse with deep, forceful thrusts. He knew Curran's chest must be raking over the rough stone walls of the natural pool with each movement, but the knowledge didn't slow him down. The warrior had asked to be well and truly fucked, so by the Gods, Tanis would fuck him to within an inch of his life.

He shifted his grip to steady Curran's hips and pummeled the young man's arse with his rigid shaft, relishing the gasps that came each time he plowed into the well-muscled flesh.

"Oh, yes, fuck me," Curran said, his voice elevated to rapturous levels.

Climax started to build at the bottom of his sexual well. Tanis leaned forward to curve his hands around the young man's shoulders. Reduced to acting the rutting beast, Tanis took a bite of the flesh at the nape of Curran's neck. Grunting, groaning, straining, Tanis experienced the most spectacular release of his life.

Plunging yet deeper, semen erupted from the end of his cock. He did call out then, but he wasn't sure that he had formed words, so thorough was the disconnect between body and brain. The only sense that registered was in his overloaded pleasure center.

His vision darkened around the edges as aftershocks continued to ripple through his system. He struggled against the loss of consciousness as he set his lover free.

"Do you still count yourself among the living, Tanis?"

The concern in Curran's voice more than his words caused Tanis to gather his wits. "Aye, though you did near kill me, I admit."

He heard the water rushing down the guardsman's body as Curran levered himself out of the pool. Tanis grimaced as he saw the red marks he'd left upon the young man's smooth, pale flesh. There would be bruises in several places come morning. However, the worst of it came from a ring of bloody imprints at the base of the man's neck. Teeth marks, his own.

"I hurt you."

"It is nothing," Curran replied, slipping into his homespun tunic.

"I am sorry for it."

The guardsman stilled his movements and fixed Tanis with a bright gaze that reflected the silvery moonlight. "I am not sorry for any of it."

Tanis' breast swelled with relief. The last thing he wanted was to repay Curran's kindness by leaving a scar that would eat away at his innocence.

Curran finished dressing in a hasty and slipshod manner. When done, he dropped to his knees beside the pool and beckoned Tanis over to him. "This is not the way I would have our time together to end."

Instantly, Tanis became alert, reacting to the change in tone. Here was no longer the playful puppy, but the guard dog going about his duty. "What do you mean?"

"To run from you like a thief in the night. But I must. It is not as easy to leave the grounds as I claimed. The sun will be up shortly, and I must be found in my own bed when the Captain comes to rouse us."

With bittersweet acceptance, Tanis replied, "Go then. I will not be the cause of trouble for you."

"Until next time, then." Surprise had Tanis' lips frozen motionless as the guardsman lowered his mouth for a goodbye kiss. Curran backed away as doubt clouded his youthful face. "Unless you would rather not set eyes on me again?"

Embarrassed, although not quite sure why, Tanis said, "Foolish pup. Why waste your time with this leathery old hide? There are far better men than me for the likes of you."

"It is you that I want, old man."

Even as his heart yearned to respond in kind, Tanis knew he should not. Such words from him would likely send them both to hell, especially if they continued to play under the Duke's nose. Far kinder to hold his tongue now than to ruin Curran's future.

"'Twas good you were, but not so good that I would pine to have you again."

Tanis thought he managed to sound convincing, but he failed to look Curran in the eye as he said it. A fatal miscalculation. Once again, he'd underestimated the young man's power of observation.

"You lie. Tell me with your kiss that you do not want me."

Tanis knew he'd fail that test. Even if he managed some measure of restraint, the warrior would sense his need.

As he struggled to find a way to evade the trap, Athena's shrill cry rent the night air. This call he knew all too well.

"Intruders approach," he hissed at the guardsman. "Take cover."

Chapter Four
~ *The Evil That Men Do* ~

Curran stood his ground and reached for the hilt of his short sword. "I will not leave you unprotected."

Under other circumstances, Tanis would have laughed at being called defenseless. Barehanded and without a coat of steel, he could kill almost any living thing. But that wasn't the sort of trouble he suspected they were about to have. "I can see to my own defense. Be gone. Now!"

The faint jangle of metal warned that they were out of time. He grabbed the guardsman by the collar and brought his face down to eye level. "Next time I tell you to run, boy, you do it."

Stubbornly, Curran shook his head. "Not if my leaving puts you in more danger."

"I will kill you myself if you disobey me again." Tanis meant every word. Some fates were far worse than death and he would spare Curran all of those if he could.

His grim face and rock-steady determination finally got through to the young man. "Understood."

"Good, now keep your mouth shut and agree with every word I say as if it came straight from your God himself."

Tanis released the fabric as a collection of armored riders emerged from the wood. The man at the front was easy to identify. Even if the crest on his shield hadn't given him away, the lordly bearing and air of command would have.

"Ah, it seems we were expected after all. How fortunate that two of my loyal subjects have ventured down to this private pool in the middle of the night to ready my bath." The Duke gazed upon Tanis with a deceptively mild expression. "That is what you are doing down here, is it not, hunt master?"

"You know how I like to keep it warm for you, Luthias," Tanis replied with lazy indifference.

Curran's sharp gasp was covered by the sound of ten swords being freed from their scabbards. There was a meaty thunk as the guardsman's short sword bit into the soil. Out of the corner of his eye, Tanis could see that the weapon was dropped vertically so the hilt rested within easy reach. Perhaps the guardsman wasn't quite so naïve as he'd first appeared.

"Oh, put your weapons away, men. I am certain my hunt master meant no offense. After all, we can hardly expect a man who lives with animals to behave as if he is better than one."

The insult glanced off Tanis' tough hide. He long ago gave up caring what the Duke thought of him. However, he did bow his head slightly in acknowledgment of the rebuke. Luthias would demand that much obedience from him at least.

"Who's the boy?"

"One of your wife's elite. I was about to send him on his way with a bug in his ear."

The Duke studied Curran for a minute. Tanis wasn't sure what had given him away, but Luthias' next question assured him that he had betrayed his feelings for the young man. Either that, or the Duke had taken a liking to the guardsman on his own. Either possibility portended equally bad results.

"Your name, boy?"

"Curran Aurick, your Grace."

"Well, Curran Aurick, do you have permission to be out of barracks so late?"

"No, your Grace."

"I see." The Duke made a production of pondering the ramifications of the violation. Finally, he said, "As I am freshly home from witnessing more horrors than one man should have to see, I find I am unable to be as stern as the situation demands. Men, please escort Curran to the keep. He is to remain in Gavin's room until I choose to release him."

One of his knights protested the order. "Your Grace, forgive me, but surely you do not mean for us to leave you here unprotected?"

Anger painted a sneer across the Duke's face. "If there ever comes a time that I fear to walk freely on my own land—and I vow to God that such a time will not come as long as I draw breath—I assure you I will take appropriate steps to cover my own arse. Now carry out my orders before I find reason to bar you from entering the castle at all."

Tanis had no chance to whisper a word of warning to Curran as he grabbed his sword and followed the mounted men up the dirt trail that led back to the castle. He doubted the young man would have heeded his counsel anyway. His eagerness to please his Grace had been evident each time Luthias spoke. Poor, unlucky sod.

Then Tanis noted a detail that had escaped him before. The Duke normally traveled with twelve men, a legacy of the roundtable knights that Luthias superstitiously thought would protect him against the Celts' attacks. At present, there were only ten. Two riderless horses trailed after the last man up the hill. Most of the men had kept to the edge of the trees. Moonlight had cast shadows upon their faces, shielding their identity. Who among Luthias' innermost circle had not made it home alive?

The Duke dismounted and ground-hitched his warhorse. As he wrested his hands free of the steel gauntlets, he said, "I see you have discovered my closest ranks have been lessened by two."

"Who?"

Luthias continued as if the question had never been asked. "The casualties were heavy this time. Some will speak against me for risking so many lives. I would counter, however, that we left behind a greater number of dead godless raiders so the sacrifice was not in vain. It will be some time before they rally enough men to strike against the might of England again."

"Who?" Tanis repeated. Fear as to the answer chilled him far more thoroughly than the steam from the hot spring could counteract.

"Sir Kloven. Damn fine man, but not the best fighter. He was lost early on in the campaign."

Tanis knew little about him, other than Gavin had been the one to champion him as a candidate for joining the Duke's tight ranks. "And the other?"

"Gavin," Luthias said shortly.

The Duke managed to free the buckles holding on the leg pieces. They fell to the ground in a noisy clatter. It was nothing compared to the angry buzzing in Tanis' head. "Gavin is dead?"

Luthias nodded. "A great loss, to be sure. His death came at a most fortuitous time, however. His end became a rallying point. Without that inspiration, I doubt any of us would have made it out of the last engagement alive. Instead, we turned the tide and chased those soulless bastards back into the hills where they belong."

Gavin. Dead. The reality of it had no substance in Tanis' existence. He needed to know more. "How? How did he die?"

"Oh, bravely, you may be assured." The Duke huffed in exasperation as his fat fingers failed to free the breastplate. "Come see to these bindings, will you? They are too tight for me to loosen from this angle."

Tanis launched himself out of the water. Naked and dripping from every possible point, he advanced on Luthias. "Tell me how he died."

"The camp minstrels crafted a song about it. Bloody, useless idiots sing it endlessly. You will hear a thousand different versions of the tale before the month is out, I am sure."

"Give me no tales. I want the truth."

Tanis wrenched at the tight fastenings, aware that if he didn't find something for his hands to do, they'd end up around the Duke's throat. As enjoyable as that act would be, he'd be taking his own life as well. There were ten witnesses, eleven counting Curran, who knew the man last in Luthias' company. And though there were many times he'd longed for death to strike him down, he'd not ever stand for it to come about in this fashion.

The last strap came free, the steel chimed like a death knoll. Luthias heaved a sigh of relief. "The truth is seldom palatable."

Tanis refused to back down, physically or verbally. "Tell me."

"Gavin's last command decision was quite foolhardy. He led his charge at a pace that far outstripped others in the field. He took a good number with him as he went down swinging, but one of those Celtic animals gored him through the heart before any of us could reach him."

Tanis assessed what he saw in the Duke's steady gaze. "You did not even try to save him."

"Well, I do admit that my unit was closest, but we were engaged. I had no free swords to send to his rescue."

Still trying to comprehend the magnitude of such a betrayal, Tanis said, "You stood by and watched him die. He was your lover, and yet you did nothing to save him."

"It had been several months since Gavin had chosen to warm my bed. I assure you, I no longer considered him my lover by the time he died." Luthias removed the rust-stained padding and other undergarments until he was stripped bare.

Tanis rocked back on his heels, his world spinning.

Words continued to spill from the Duke's mouth. "I demand unswerving loyalty from my men. All who take the oath understand this. Gavin wavered. I no longer had an obligation to watch over him. It was his own choice, Tanis."

"You filthy, despicable offspring of a goat." Tanis backed Luthias into a tree, a sinewy forearm pressed against the Duke's throat. The impact shook the leaves all the way up to the very top. "Gavin loved you."

"Once, perhaps. But then he chose Kloven over me. I could not have that."

"Your damn pride will one day kill us all. I should end your life now and spare the few innocents who believe a human heart still beats in your empty breast." Tanis raised his arm to strike a killing blow with naught more than his hammer-like fist.

"No one lives forever, and eventually my time too will come. However, remember that if my death should come at your hands, there is more than yourself who will pay the price."

No, Tanis hadn't forgotten that, although the implications of extracting revenge for Gavin's murder—and it was murder, surely as if Luthias had held the killing sword himself—hadn't completely filtered through his mind. But now that the connection had been made between act and punishment, Tanis' hands were tied. He let the Duke go, watching as the man nonchalantly returned to the pool.

"Fate will see that you pay a high price for your treachery, Luthias."

"Perhaps." The Duke lowered himself into the steaming water. "Young Curran looks a lot like Gavin at his age, do you agree?"

Please, no. Not the sweet rascal Curran. Hadn't the man ruined enough lives for one lifetime? "I did not study him that closely."

Luthias fingered the earth that had been roughened during Curran's violent release. "He looks quite the capable sort. Now that there is room in my inner circle, I will have to see if he meets my standards."

"He is soft from guarding your simple-minded wife. Too soft for your tastes, I am sure."

"I thought you did not get a good look at him."

Tanis silently cursed himself. He never should have strayed into the clearing. His company brought nothing but misery of one kind or another to those he met under the moonlight. "I know his duties well enough."

"Speaking of duties, I think it is time that you see to your own. I am sure my people will want to celebrate my victorious return."

Tanis bundled his clothes under his arm, then left the small clearing without so much as a backward glance. By the Gods, he prayed he would live to see the day that Luthias paid for his many sins. Until then there was naught he could do but continue to lead the solitary life that kept meat on his Grace's table and his head off the executioner's chopping block.

And try to forget about Gavin, Curran and any chance at happiness he might have had.

Overhead, Athena soared, releasing the wail that he could not permit to escape his aching, heavy chest.

C3 80 80

Curran paced the confines of Sir Gavin's quarters as dawn's blush receded, leaving the sky a bright blue. No one had come to explain why he was being detained, and a locked door prevented him from wandering out to find answers on his own. He wondered what he'd done to deserve such treatment, for surely if he were to be punished for cleansing himself in the Duke's private waters they'd be holding him in a cell, not in these lavish rooms.

Yet he couldn't think of another transgression that would warrant a personal dressing-down by the Duke's most trusted advisor. Not that Curran considered himself an altar boy. But he'd certainly know if he'd done something so offensive as to require a tongue-lashing from Sir Gavin, wouldn't he?

This question drove him crazy all morning. He couldn't sleep for fear of being caught napping when he should be vigilant, respectful of all things that were not rightly his. When the time for the noonday meal arrived, judging by the grumblings of his empty stomach, there finally came a knock at the door.

Curran couldn't open it, but did call for the servant on the other side to enter. It had to be a servant as no one of the noble class would think to alert the occupants of a room before they strode in, certainly not within their own castle.

There was another round of muffled banging before the door opened. Evander, one of the higher-ranking servants in the castle, fell through the opening, landing on the huge burden he carried in his arms.

Curran hurried over to the man and helped him to his feet. "Are you hurt?"

"Nay, sir. I be old and clumsy, 'tis all."

"What have you brought there?" The bundle had been wrapped in Curran's own cloak.

"Your belongings, sir."

"Am I to be dismissed from service then?"

Evander shook his iron grey capped head. "'Tis not for me to say, young sir. I was told to fetch your things from the home guard's barracks and leave them here. More I do not know."

The old servant kept his head bowed, avoiding Curran's eyes. Although servants showed more respect toward others while in the royal chambers, they usually relaxed around the guards when left alone. Evander was one of the few Curran counted as a friend. He didn't understand why Evander suddenly spoke to him with such formality.

Curran kneeled on the floor and inspected his possessions to see if anything had been left behind. "They are too heavy for one man to carry alone. You should have asked for help."

Evander backed up, his eyes still on the floor. "I alone serve this room. That is the way the Duke wishes it."

Several questions sprang to mind but the servant vanished before Curran could utter one. In the silence that followed Evander's departure, he could clearly hear the sound of the lock slipping back into place.

"Imprisoned once more," Curran said aloud though there was no one but himself to hear.

The contents of the bundle were wrapped with some amount of care. Even so, he noted his pewter mug had a new dent, his favorite spoon bent. There was a pair of drawers that didn't seem to be his, but since they had a small coin in the pocket he wasn't going to cast them aside.

The dent in the cup though...

The door opened after a turn of the lock. Assuming it was Evander returning with another delivery, Curran continued to rummage through the items on the floor. "Shall I remain bent over, my good man, so that you may aim a well-placed kick to my backside as it appears you have already done to my best cup?"

The clearing of a masculine throat caused Curran to look up. He needed no more than a glimpse of the fancy black boots to know he was speaking irreverently to one of a station well above that of a house servant.

If his goose hadn't been cooked before, it surely was now.

Chapter Five
~ *A Tarnished Proposal* ~

"I beg your pardon, your Grace. I mean no disrespect." Curran stayed on his knees, his head bowed until he was doubled over.

"Rise, Curran, and face me like a man."

Trembling, Curran stood, shoulders squared. For no reason he could fathom, he happened to notice that he and the Duke were about the same height, putting Tanis slightly taller than them both. "How may I serve you, your Grace?"

Instead of responding, Luthias leaned down and picked up the pitiful excuse for a drinking cup. "A servant treated your belongings with such disrespect? Who was it?"

"An accident, your Grace. No harm done, really."

"Accident or not, any servant that tends to you should treat your possessions as if they are as precious to him as his own hide. I will have his name from you."

Curran didn't want to further upset the Duke who was now looking at the cup with something akin to anger.

Why was Luthias making such a fuss over a cheap cup? It couldn't possibly mean anything to him.

"It was Evander, Duke Luthias, but I—"

The older man waved him to silence with a gloved hand. He set the cup down on the washstand as gently as if it were a fragile piece of glass. "Do you know why you are here, Curran?"

"Because your Grace requested that it be so," he replied, certain that was the only correct answer.

"Yes, yes, but do you know why I asked for *you* to be brought *here*?"

Mutely, Curran shook his head. His blond curls tumbled over his forehead, but he refused to move to brush them away.

"Do you like this room?"

Curran wondered at the second abrupt change in topic but answered, "Very much, sir."

In truth, it was a small white lie. Overall, the chamber was nice enough but it had far too many frills for Curran's comfort. The chamber was heavily draped in red and gold fabric, and the furniture got in his way if he wanted to pace the length of the room. He much preferred the barracks where the straw bedding he'd claimed for himself had arranged itself into the perfect nest for his body, where he didn't have to worry about breaking a trinket or getting dirt on fine linen every time he wanted to sit down.

"Would you like to lodge here?"

To be jailed here permanently? What would Sir Gavin then do for a room? Surely the Duke had something else in mind. "I do not understand the question, your Grace."

"This." Luthias gestured to encompass the entire room. "Would you like all this to be yours?"

Curran frowned. Was this some kind of trick? "This room belongs to your most loyal knight, Sir Gavin."

"Not anymore." Luthias crossed the room to the window and looked out upon his land. "Sir Gavin Andrew died a warrior's death during this last campaign, slain by the animal raiders from the North."

Suddenly Curran's knees went weak and he felt like slipping to the floor. He took courage from the Duke's straight spine and remained upright, drawing in one breath after another as he tried to work around the lump in his throat. Sir Gavin was the best and brightest of all the Duke's knights. If the Celts had downed one so mighty as him, then what hope remained for the rest of them?

"Your Grace, I can scarcely believe it."

"I assure you there is no mistake. Gavin is dead."

How sad, to lose his closest friend so swiftly, so brutally. Though he hid his grief well, Luthias must be pained to the core. There was little Curran could do to offer comfort. Even the simplest touch was forbidden without Luthias' permission. "I grieve for your loss, your Grace, as I am sure does all who knew him."

The Duke seemed not to hear or want this offer of sympathy. "So, you see, Curran, this room has no one to claim it. It can be yours, if you wish it."

51

To take the place of Sir Gavin? Was the Duke so grief-stricken that he'd lost his wits? It was the embodiment of Curran's most cherished dream, to be sure, but he'd done nothing to earn it. "It is a great honor that you should think me worthy, your Grace, but there are far more qualified men than I to sit at your side and give you good counsel."

The Duke turned. Although his face still looked composed, his voice was now thickened by strong emotion. "You look so much like him."

Others in the castle had remarked on the resemblance, so Curran wasn't surprised by the observation. However, that the Duke had said so now made him uneasy. With the Duke's men in residence, Curran's services wouldn't be needed to guard the Duchess until they again took leave. That should make it easy to avoid putting himself in front of the Duke where his visage might bring pain.

Slowly, Curran said, "I take that as a great compliment, sir, but if it distresses you I shall do my best to stay out of your sight until such time as you give me leave to serve you."

Again the Duke behaved as if he hadn't heard a word Curran had spoken. The older man closed the distance between them. He reached out to caress Curran's cheek with the back of his hand. Heat was palpable through the leather, the scent of horses still clinging to the supple hide from the long ride home.

"I spoke with Tanis after you left. He also thinks you are much like my dear Gavin."

Curran was stunned by the gesture. He'd oft dreamed of having the Duke look at him the way he was now, with such warmth and yearning in his eyes. Yet the feeling was uncomfortable, knowing that the look stemmed, in part, from Luthias' feelings for a dead man. "Is that why you are offering me his quarters? Because I resemble him?"

Luthias dropped his hand and resumed a businesslike tone. "I do not need to explain myself to you. Accept that I have a need which you are uniquely qualified to fill. However, there are conditions if you choose to accept. Are you prepared to hear them?"

Though he was loath to take advantage of a situation granted him by the death of such a noble man, he couldn't help but be excited. In time, he would prove himself worthy of the honor he vowed. "I am, your Grace."

"You will swear fealty to me."

"I already have, your Grace. When I took up arms in defense of your castle, your property and your kin."

"To me," the Duke repeated. "Not to the crown I wear."

An unusual request, one usually reserved for members of the Duke's household and those he wished to have fight under his banner. It meant forsaking all others, including any in his line who might one day succeed him. Curran would have to give it careful consideration. "So noted."

"Secondly, you would no longer be a caretaker for the Duchess. You would become my squire, riding at my side into battle."

This was the chance Curran had been hoping for. Not that it would come about in quite this manner, but he was eager to prove his worth, test his mettle on the battlefield rather than a practice field. To serve in a position of honor. He never dreamed such an opportunity would come so soon, or with such ease.

"Understood."

"And you would also share my bed."

His *bed*?

Curran pinched his own arm, hard. Pain proved he wasn't dreaming, but this moment hardly felt real. As he watched the red flush of blood rush in to fill the whiteness on his arm, he said, "I fear I did not hear you correctly, your Grace."

The Duke chuckled. "You heard me right enough. Gavin did the same when I asked him. Pinching his arm like a child with fairy dust in his eyes."

"You are asking me to become your lover?" Saying the words didn't make the situation any more real to him. His heart beat so fast he was growing lightheaded.

But instead of being full of warm anticipation as he had been with Tanis, Curran tingled with nervousness before the Duke. He had so few lovers, so little practice in the art of pleasing men.

"My lover, my confidant, my squire. All that and much more, once you accept."

Emotion clogged Curran's brain. He couldn't think, couldn't even slow his thoughts to where he could recognize them beyond a general blur. Was this madness? "I do not know what to say."

"You could say yes," Luthias prompted him, his brown eyes smiling.

Curran shook his head. "You honor me beyond all my expectations. I need time to decide if I am worthy."

Anger brought a deep furrow to Duke Luthias' brow. "Shall I order you, spare you the burden of decision-making?"

Lest the Duke get the wrong impression, Curran explained, "I do not fear the making of the choice, your Grace. I wish only to look upon my soul and see if I am worthy of what you propose."

"I am your Duke. Do you not trust me to know my own mind and what is best for those who serve me?"

"Without question," Curran replied promptly. "It is just that my mind until now has been shielded from you by position and circumstance. I would not burden you with a heart flawed or a courage weakened by such a fortuitous reversal of fortune."

"You sound like one of those popinjays my wife fancies."

Curran frowned at the mention of the Duchess. "And what of your lady wife, your Grace? I should not want my presence to cause a rift between you."

"She accepted Gavin's presence in my private affairs and she will accept you. You have my word on it."

Despite the reassurance, Curran was uncertain. He had been quite honest when he told Luthias he wanted to make sure that such a swift, dramatic rise in station would not malign his good judgment and sense of fair play.

"I see you are not convinced. I have to say although I am disappointed, I am not surprised. Gavin declined me twice before I managed to convince him otherwise."

Curran's unruly cock, though previously well spent, twitched over thoughts of how Duke Luthias could have persuaded a young Gavin.

A trace of lust must have crossed his face for the Duke closed the gap between them. This time, instead of a touch of his gloved hand, the older man breathed across Curran's lips. "Do you require some small demonstration of my esteem for you?"

"Whatever your Grace wishes."

Curran held his breath in anticipation. The effort was wasted as the first touch of Luthias' lips stole what little air he had left. Greedily nibbling along the bottom edge of Curran's mouth, the Duke moaned his enjoyment of this simple act.

As if captured in the effect of an evil spell, Curran couldn't move. His arms stayed at his sides as if bound by iron braces. It would mean his life to touch the Duke's person without permission.

"Do you find my attentions so unpleasant that you must force yourself to stand still and submit to them?" the Duke demanded hotly.

"Your Grace," Curran said, near frustrated tears, "I wish to pleasure you in every way I can name and a few that do not yet have one, but you have not given me leave to do so. I will not violate your person to satisfy my own selfish needs."

Luthias lowered his head. When his eyes came up to meet with Curran's once more, they were filled with wry amusement. "It has been some time since I have asked a new lover into my bed that I have forgotten the rules which you must otherwise obey."

"Release me or send me away, but do not keep my desires trapped within my own body like this," Curran begged, nearly at the end of his ability to restrain himself.

The Duke licked Curran's upper lip.

The resulting shock of lust went straight to Curran's loins. His shaft hardened and his breath expelled from his chest in coarse gasps. "Please, your Grace. I beg of you."

"Show me then, young Curran. Give me your kiss and let me feel how much you want to please me."

Curran had no chance to move before Luthias was on him. Near brutal kisses seared him as the Duke pressed him backward toward the bed. The thick oak frame held him upright as he matched the older man's intensity, dueling with lips and tongue instead of wicked, sharp blades.

Despite the Duke's maturity, his cock rose tall and strong inside his breeches. Curran flexed his thigh, giving Luthias a hard surface to grind against. His own rod quivered with anticipation of what might come next.

But just as Curran was gathering his courage to caress the older man, to bring his proud erection out where it could be admired, the Duke pulled away, leaving a yard of emptiness between them.

"You tempt me beyond what is safe in the daylight," Luthias told him, wiping dampness from the corner of his mouth.

"If I do so, it is because of you that I am so inspired."

"Then shall I take your enthusiasm as a sign of your agreement?"

Several heartbeats passed as Curran tried to marshal his scattered thoughts.

The Duke grew impatient and said, "You are no more eager to jump into this arrangement now than you were before. I would curse you for it if I did not understand so well that your feelings are based on honorable qualities, the very same qualities I so admired in Gavin. I was right to ask you to join my household and my bed, but I dislike waiting."

"Will you give me some time to consider my worthiness for your offer?"

"Yes."

Curran's relief was so great that he nearly wet himself. Struggling to maintain an expressionless demeanor now that they were back on less personal ground, he said, "I shall endeavor to be quick as well as thorough in my deliberations."

"You would be wise to be both," the Duke replied. He crossed the room until he once again stood between the door and the washbasin. "In three days' time, after a suitable mourning period for the loss of my favored knight, this castle will host a victory celebration. Between now and then, you shall remain secluded in this chamber. You will not be permitted any visitors save for a servant to bring your meals."

Three *days*? He'd been hoping for no more than a few hours. "How shall I let you know I have reached a decision?"

"I shall come to you. Once the revelers have taken to their beds, I will knock upon your door but once. If you admit me, I will take it to mean you accept the terms of my offer. Should you fail to let me in, for any reason, you will be dismissed from my service."

Curran acknowledged this ultimatum with a slight bow. "As you desire, your Grace."

Duke Luthias paused in the act of reaching for the lever to release the catch. He picked up the damaged pewter mug, considering it. Speaking to it more than to its owner, he said, "Sometimes one is tempted to keep hold of the past like a frightened child clinging to its mother's skirts. A man willing to walk away from all he knows is worth more to me than a hundred children and shall know his worth in no small means." With care, he upended the cup and placed it on the edge of the tabletop. In one mighty stroke, he crushed it under his fist. "Those unable to take that first small, brave step shall see the other side of me."

Long after the door closed behind the Duke, Curran gazed at the flat metal disk and reflected on his future.

Chapter Six
~ *Coming to Terms* ~

Hours passed in agonizing slowness, yet the day of the feast dawned far more quickly than Curran thought possible. Though weak from hunger, for the Duke had ordered him put on reduced rations so that his heart could speak more closely with God, he felt strong-minded and confident about his choice.

Since he felt certain Luthias wouldn't come to him before late evening, Curran passed the daylight hours in front of his only window, gazing down upon the busy area behind the kitchen where extra cooking fires had been lit. When the wind blew from the north, heavenly aromas tickled Curran's nose. Deer, fowl and hare caught by Tanis roasted on several spits, their juices dripping to sizzle on the hot embers.

Tanis. Odd how often the hunt master came to mind. Then again, perhaps it wasn't so odd after all. The night with Tanis figured largely in Curran's deliberations. To dedicate himself to Luthias in mind, body and soul meant that there would be no other opportunity to savor the sensual delights the hunter had to give.

Wet, hungry kisses. Lean, strong arms. A stiff cock that—

"Enough," Curran told himself sternly as his own rod hardened at the memories of how good it had felt to be the recipient of Tanis' forceful thrusts.

No doubt his ardor had more to do with the dearth of physical love in the preceding months than any special talents the hunt master possessed. Surely his body would react with equal passion when Luthias came to visit. For, after taking all other aspects into consideration, Curran had decided to admit the Duke when he knocked.

Curran thought the night would hover on the edge of forever, creeping up on him only when his back was turned. As it turned out, he had little chance to notice the passing of the day. Evander entered the room a bit earlier than had been his usual custom. His arms were laden with a morning repast fit for a king.

"His Grace asks that you enjoy this hearty meal," the servant told Curran, still addressing the floor.

As hungry as he was, it was the servant who drew his attention. This dog-in-the-manger behavior had gone on long enough. "Why will you not look me in the eye when you speak to me, Evander? We used to be friends."

"I would rather not say, my Lord."

"Lord? What rubbish is that? I am no more noble born than you."

The servant settled the tray upon the large, square chest at the foot of the bed. "The Duke has announced to those within the keep that he has taken you into his family. You are to be treated the same as we would treat any member of his direct line."

Holy fuck! It was only because he covered his mouth that this curse did not ring throughout the valley. Curran couldn't be more surprised. Then his brain caught up with his heart and he realized that Evander had cleverly thrown out this information in an attempt to distract him from the previous question.

"You avoid the issue, Evander. Even though I am to be treated as a noble now, we were first friends. Have I done something to wrong you?"

"Not in such a manner as you would recognize, my Lord."

What in the Seven Hells was he going on about? "Speak plainly, man. I have not the patience to whittle my way through your convoluted thoughts."

"'Tis worth my life to do so," Evander admitted, glancing over his shoulder at the open door.

Curran strode across the room and slammed it shut. He then went to the window where he closed the heavy drapes. Although more secrecy shouldn't be necessary, he grabbed Evander by the collar and brought him to the center of the room, away from any wall where a lack of mortar could provide a spy-hole.

"Speak now to me in low tones. I give you my word that I will not repeat what you share."

The servant then replied in a voice so soft that Curran had to strain to hear him even though they were standing nose to nose. "Evil lives within these stones, my Lord. A

63

dark and dangerous madness infects the most respected of men. 'Tis only a matter of time until you succumb to the same disease, and I wish not to see it overtake you as it has claimed so many others."

"Evil? Madness? What nonsense you speak."

Evander hunched his shoulders in defeat. "You are blinded to it, yet I swear to you it exists. I have seen great men fall prey to its all-consuming power. I wish you had never been brought here."

"Duke Luthias is a man of noble blood and noble heart. Surely he would not tolerate such defilement within his keep."

"Do not speak his name," the servant hissed. "Lest you call his attention to you."

"You say that as if the Duke has the powers of a devil, to know all, to see that which he could not possibly see."

"That man is the very creature of which you speak. I have seen him engage in acts to sicken your soul. A monster who delights in blood, who fornicates with his own kind, who defiles the very house he claims is pure with these atrocities."

Ah. Curran gained a glimmer of understanding. Servants were often a superstitious lot. Lovemaking between men, particularly by those who did not share the taste, could be construed as a sacrilegious act. A bias that, in truth, was held by more than the commoners and fueled Curran's caution not to let his true feelings for the Duke be known.

And then there were those who could not reconcile their needs with their moral beliefs and thus tortured themselves and their partner in the process. If Evander had witnessed such an act inside the castle walls, it would explain much.

But how to convey that to Evander without giving himself away?

"Sometimes what we see has a hidden meaning that cannot be disclosed to the naked eye," Curran told the servant who now trembled under his hand.

"So you say, my Lord, and so I think you mean. But Sir Gavin told me otherwise shortly before his departure, and *he did not come back.*"

This new information troubled Curran as he could not see how it fit with his theory. The Duke had told him of his special relationship with the knight. No doubt, as sole caretaker of the room and its occupant, Evander had come upon them at a time when they were too involved with each other to notice. Perhaps when confronted with what Evander had seen, Gavin replied with this preposterous story of madness and wicked sin to ensure that the servant would speak of it to no other.

Unfortunately, there was no opportunity to test this new conjecture as there came another knock at the door.

On this day more than any other, Curran could not let a summons go unanswered. He remembered well the Duke's warning. "Yes? Who is there?"

The door swung open revealing two lads struggling to keep a wide, wooden tub upright on its side. As they muscled it through the opening, Evander moved away so as not to look like they had been in close conference. "My Lord, forgive me for not making myself heard when I spoke of this earlier. To close the drapes as you ordered done summoned your bath."

Trying not to laugh at the way the young boys wrestled with the tub tied Curran's stomach into one big knot. As tempted as he was to help them, he stood idly by as any other noble in the castle would have done. If he had indeed been admitted to the Duke's family, he would not dishonor them by acting in a manner unbefitting his new station.

He couldn't prevent himself from having a bit of fun with Evander though to relieve their previous tension. "So am I expected to drown myself every night as I close the drapes before bed?"

"Not unless that is what my Lord wishes. This morning the arrangement was made at the Duke's request. Again I beg your pardon that I did not make my meaning clear."

Clear? It hadn't been mentioned at all. Not that Curran blamed the man for this neglect. Curran hadn't given him the chance. "Right. A bath. I seem to recall you saying some such thing. Well, so be it. Fill it up, boys. The day wears on."

There. That sounded pompous enough.

Evander looked a bit started by the transformation, but hurried after the young ones to oversee the carrying of the water. No doubt, more would end up on themselves and the floor than would remain in the pail if left to their own devices.

From that point on, the day advanced at a rapid pace. Servants scurried in and out of his room like mice under Evander's catlike gaze. Curran bathed. He dressed in new finery. His bedding was changed. His old belongings were carefully packed away in a trunk.

In between activities, Curran stole bites of salted ham from the tray Evander had brought to him early on. His thoughts bounced between Tanis and Luthias, Gavin and Evander.

Finally, as dusk settled a colorful blanket over the distant hills, Curran had no more answers about this mysterious evil Gavin spoke of than when he began. Perhaps he could raise the matter with the Duke when he came to visit. He had promised Evander that his words would not be repeated, but surely there was a way to gain understanding about what had transpired without putting the servant at risk.

ରଃଡ଼ର

The knock came well past the midnight hour. Curran had finally given in to his body's need to lie down. As he rushed toward the door, he jerked at the fabric encasing his limbs, trying to arrange it as Evander had before he took his leave. "Yes? Please come in."

Curran heard the sound of iron hinges protesting yet the door before him did not move at all. How could that be?

"I knew you would make the right decision," Luthias said from behind Curran.

Curran spun around in time to see a part of the interior wall close. A part that, up until now, he'd assumed was solid rock. A secret passage, then. It thrilled his heart to learn of it. Where there was one there might be others. It was the kind of thing that could be useful to know.

"I see you have donned garments suitable to your new station," Luthias observed, stepping further into the room. "Do you like them?"

Curran noticed the man was a little unsteady on his feet. "They take some getting used to, your Grace. All this"—he gestured at the room, flapping his arms like a bird—"seems excessive."

The Duke laughed. "That's what being rich is all about, my young friend. Being excessive."

Luthias rested against the bed. Even in the dim light, Curran could see desire in the man's eyes. He waited for the hitch of sexual yearning to drop into the pit of his belly, but it didn't come. Had nerves cowed his libido into retreat?

"Come here, boy."

Curran winced at the term. He didn't want to be seen as a child, especially not now. However, he approached the Duke with proper humility. "Yes, your Grace?"

Luthias hooked a greasy hand around his neck. Curran could smell the remains of the feast from that close touch. "Are you prepared to give me a demonstration of your gratitude?"

"Of course, your Grace. I owe you much."

"Then see to it."

The older man tugged on his neck, encouraging him to bend. Curran required no additional coaching to know what was expected of him. However, the Duke seemed far too deep in his cups to remain upright while Curran was otherwise engaged. "Perhaps you would be more comfortable if you were to lay down," he suggested.

Luthias glanced over his shoulder toward the bed, then curled his fingers as if seeking the stem of a cup. "No," he bit out harshly. "On your knees, now. Pay proper homage to me, or the deal is off."

Curran did as he was asked. He resented the way the Duke was approaching what should be a special time, but he knew he should be grateful for every scrap of attention Luthias threw his way. It would be all too easy to end up back in the barracks—or worse, out of the castle entirely—before he got his first taste of battle.

It turned out that there was a use for all that fabric, as it cushioned his bones, preventing his knees from resting against the hard stone floor. He reached for the Duke's breeches. There was no hardness to be found under his fingers.

Luthias would find the same if he were to search for evidence of Curran's lust. Somehow, that made it even more difficult for Curran to proceed. With Tanis, each movement had been so natural. So easy. So welcome. Tonight, with the Duke, Curran would be little better than a hired whore.

Ah, Tanis, why couldn't it be you in my bedchamber tonight?

"Do I not interest you?"

Curran's head snapped back as the Duke roughly tugged on his hair. He could see Luthias' eyes clouding with anger. "No, your Grace. It is awe and respect that slow my hands."

To his relief, the Duke chuckled and released him. "I thought Tanis would have disabused you of any such romantic notions when it came to me."

"Truthfully, your Grace, the hunt master had not spoken much to me before you came upon us."

The Duke caressed Curran's head, petting him like a beloved hound. For some reason, it set Curran's teeth on edge.

"Then he is not your lover?"

Confident that the candlelight would conceal any trace of deception, Curran said, "I have never visited his bed, nor he mine."

"That is not the question I asked, boy. Has he claimed you as his lover?"

"No, your Grace." For in truth, Tanis had not. Although they had taken each other, the hunt master had not spoken any words of claim. If anything, Tanis had protested the opposite.

To distract the Duke from his current topic, Curran fumbled with the lacings to expose Luthias' member. It was flaccid and far from sweet smelling. Curran used the softest cuff of his sleeve to clean it off under the guise of sexual stimulation.

The Duke seemed not to notice and continued with his discussion. "What if I told you I heard otherwise as we came upon you?"

"I would say you have excellent hearing, your Grace."

Luthias' lengthening rod twitched within Curran's fist. "Then you admit he favors you?"

"No, your Grace. I meant the words that drifted to you upon the wind must have been uttered some greater distance away as the hunt master never said as much to me."

The Duke got a cold look in his eye. "You have a smart mouth on you, boy. Let us see if you are as good with my cock as you are with words."

Curran dutifully applied his teeth and tongue to the job of arousing the Duke. Luthias' member flopped around his mouth like a dying fish. Curran moaned in dismay.

None of his fantasies about the Duke had proceeded like this. In all his dreams, the Duke's rod jutted out straight and proud. His skin was sweet tasting and not nearly so pliant. In fact, it was much more like loving Tanis had been.

Dwelling on the hunt master increased his enthusiasm. The Duke seemed to appreciate his renewed efforts and was eventually brought to completion. When Luthias spilled his seed, it was a piteous amount, a fact which made it possible for Curran to swallow the sour substance without gagging.

"Now I know you were speaking the truth," Luthias said as he tucked his limp and sticky member away. "Tanis would have trained you better if you had been his for any length of time."

Curran sat back on his heels. He didn't know what reaction he expected—the Duke and his kind did not often give thanks to those beneath their station—but surely he could have used words far kinder than these. "If I failed to please you, I offer my humblest apologies."

"Oh, get up, will you? I am not displeased. In fact, I think I will enjoy training you to my tastes over those of that beast."

Curran rose to his feet as the Duke retreated into the shadows in the far corner of the chamber where the hidden door lay. He hadn't expected Luthias to leave so soon. There were many questions to be answered. Ones of far more importance than the Duke had seen fit to raise. "Duke Luthias, may I ask when I might see you next?"

A chuckle came from the shadows, and Curran shivered. He could well believe that sound was responsible, at least in part, for Evander's rumors of evil. It was not the sound of a happy man, but rather of one drunk on power.

"That eager for my cock, are you, boy?"

"As your unworthy vassal, I am eager to be with you in all ways you see fit to have me."

"Another pretty speech, Curran, but I have had enough of you for one night."

"Then I shall present myself to you in the morning?" Curran pressed.

Luthias ran his hands over the stone wall. The light was too dim for Curran to see what the Duke was doing. "Though I just returned from a lengthy campaign, it seems our enemy grows braver and bolder. I must make plans to depart within a fortnight. Therefore, you will have to find other ways to amuse yourself until all is in readiness and we take our leave."

For the first time since Luthias arrived that night, Curran felt the stirrings of excitement in his chest. "Your Grace, if there is anything I can do—"

The Duke cut him off. "You have much to prove before I am willing to trust you with my most private thoughts. You can start earning that trust by remembering you belong to me now. Once I see that you can conduct yourself in the manner befitting a member of my household, I may find other tasks for you to do."

There was a slight puff of cool air as the concealed door opened. Luthias departed without another word. And once again, Curran was left alone in the dark to wonder what he had gotten himself into.

Chapter Seven
~ *Intentions* ~

Curran used every excuse he could think of to roam the castle and attendant structures. Before his activities had been limited by his position as a member of the Duchess' guard, always following in her footsteps rather than going about on his own. Now that his circumstances had changed, he had more freedom and he had every intention of putting it to good use.

He learned much about the inner workings of the keep during his explorations. His fascination with hidden things led him to scour the stone walls for more secret passages. He discovered that the one in his room was part of a network that led from the Duchess' private suite all the way down to the dungeon.

The dungeon had surprised him. There were several cells being used as storage rooms. Some contained food, but even more contained a treasure trove of expensive gifts. Enough to fund the running of Luthias' costly campaign for years to come.

What disturbed him were the two currently empty cells that showed signs of recent use. Human waste mixed with the sparse straw covering the stone floor. Living in isolation as he had for those few days, it was possible that criminals had been brought to justice without him learning of it.

Possible, but not likely.

On his way back to his room through normal channels, Evander waylaid him. The servant ducked into a recessed alcove and bid Curran to follow.

"I know it has become your habit to leave your room while the castle sleeps, m'Lord. But please, sire, do not go roaming tonight if you value your life."

"What makes you say this?"

Mournfully, Evander explained, "I have worked in this castle, for the Duke and his family, since I was a young lad. I know the secrets of these walls better than I know my own name. You would be wise to listen to me now, even if you cannot bring yourself to believe I speak the truth."

"How do you know I sometimes leave my chamber in the middle of the night?"

"I check on you throughout the darkness, as I do with all of those who are in my care."

Curran had to suppress a laugh. Evander's professed devotion to duty was an unnecessary act since each room had a bellpull to summon him if a need arose. Perhaps he just liked wandering after hours when the castle was quiet and a man could think, as Curran did.

"All right, Evander. I will spend tonight in my chamber."

Evander gave him a doubt-filled look, but only said, "From the darkest hour onward, if you value your life."

"Understood. Thank you for the warning."

Even as he spoke, he knew there was one thing he must do in order to keep his word to Duke Luthias. For several nights now, he'd considered sneaking out of the castle to find the hunt master's cabin. Though Luthias never expressly forbade him from seeking out Tanis, Curran hadn't wanted to approach the man in the daylight, lest the Duke learn of his activities and get the wrong impression.

Now, under the cover of dusk before the night grew too old, Curran knew the time had come. Surely he would be back before midnight, thus his promise to Evander wouldn't be in vain. He changed into dark clothing that wouldn't get in his way, and followed the plan he had laid out for escaping into the countryside undetected.

CB℘EO

Although Athena was not about to warn him, Tanis sensed the change in the forest as a stranger approached. Few would dare to come so deep into the trees at nightfall. His guest must be extremely foolish, or extremely brave.

Foolish, no doubt, Tanis thought. He wasn't sure if he should be joyous or angry that the young guardsman had finally decided to seek him out.

Tanis opened the door to his rustic, one room cabin, then returned to his task of chopping vegetables to add to his stew.

"Should I take this open door as a gesture of welcome?" Curran asked, his voice cheerful. It was the same tone that haunted Tanis every night in his dreams. A voice that offered pleasure, only to fade to moonbeams when he reached out to grab on with both hands.

"If that is your wish, so be it," he replied shortly.

"Have I come at a bad time?"

"No worse than any other."

Curran entered and shut the door behind him. Suddenly what had always been a room big enough to keep him from feeling confined shrank to the size of an unbearable prison. Tanis shifted his broad shoulders to assure himself that the walls were not closing in and continued to reduce the vegetables to small bits.

"What brings you?" Tanis asked, pressured into speech by the long silence.

"You."

"Luthias has turned you into an errand boy?"

"No, I come of my own accord."

Tanis considered that piece of information. More than two weeks had passed since the night they met. Why had it taken Curran so long to visit? Had Luthias poisoned the boy against him?

And why did the answers to these and a thousand other questions he wanted to ask Curran matter to him so much?

"Speak your piece then."

Slowly, Curran began, "You heard of Gavin's death?"

"Aye."

"And you know I have been staying in his rooms?"

"Aye."

"What do you make of it?"

Tanis carried the now minced carrot, onion and turnip to the boiling pot that hung on an iron hook over the fire and dumped them in. "A polished apple can conceal a rotten core."

"But the apple can also be good through and through. Is that not more likely?"

"Not when it is grown in Luthias' orchard."

"Evander would agree with you," Curran replied. "But I have no evidence of his treachery."

"Evander is a superstitious peasant, but one who knows evil. You would be wise to listen to him."

"Gloom and doom. Gloom and doom. Can no one but me be pleased about my rise in station?"

"If you want smoke blown up your arse, go to the kitchens. One of their giant bellows should be fit for the task."

Curran laughed, somehow retaining his good humor despite the seriousness of the subject. "The only thing I desire up my arse is something far more substantial than air."

Another kind of silence settled over the room. Tanis couldn't prevent his thoughts from straying to the one time he'd followed through with the very act Curran described. By the Gods, it had been good. His cock twitched, filling with desire to take seconds and thirds of what the young man had to offer.

But that was not why Curran had come. He belonged to Luthias now. Tanis had to accept that, and so did his cock.

Luckily, a soft cooing reminded him of another hunger that needed to be sated. He lifted the worn blanket that covered his bed and pulled a wire cage out from under it. A grey pigeon blinked, then cooed again.

"Dinner?"

Curran's voice sounded thick to his ears. Could it be the young man was similarly affected by their close proximity? "No," Tanis replied, having a care to keep his fingers away from the bird's sharp beak. "I came across her, injured in a fight with another of her kind. I hope to return her to her nest in another day or so."

"But why? Surely she would make you a good meal."

Tanis shrugged. "There are few good reasons to take a life. For food. For survival. Neither of which are relevant here. I have all the meat I need, and while this little one is fierce, I hardly think my life is endangered by her presence."

"So you will tend to her wounds and set her free?"

"Aye," Tanis agreed, feeling uncomfortable with the approval in Curran's voice. He only knew one way to live, and that was what he did.

He fed the pigeon, then returned her to the cage and covered her up. When he turned around, Curran was right there.

"You are a good and honorable man, Tanis of Appin."

Such a sweet and happy face Curran had. And Luthias had been right. It was also much like Gavin's when he first came to the Duke's keep. Not that it had stayed happy and innocent for long. It angered him to think of Curran suffering the same fate. If he were Duke...

But he wasn't. And that truth added to the rage burning in his chest. "You are blind!"

The young man flinched as if struck. He retreated to the other side of the room. "If you mean that I prefer to see the good in people rather than dig for the bad, then I suppose you are right."

"Nothing good in this life comes freely. What price will you be asked to pay in return for your good fortune? Have you thought of that?"

"I already know what price Luthias expects from me. My sword, my loyalty. My advice in battle. Small coin in return for all he has promised me."

That wasn't all Luthias would demand of the young man. Either the Duke left out that part of their arrangement or Curran had not yet been informed of those duties. Neither prospect pleased Tanis. "The Duke's promises have no more substance than spun sugar. Do not make the mistake of thinking he lives by the same laws you do. If it is to his advantage, he will take more than your word. He will take your bloody life."

"Aye, if need be," Curran replied with a calm acceptance.

"He is not worth it." The words came out harsh, filled with a lifetime of hatred for the man who considered his subjects as nothing more than game pieces. For the man who played with lives as if he were God.

"I would argue that as the Duke of this province, my life is in his hands whether I have given my pledge or not."

"That man is a butcher, a murderer, a soulless thief. I wish you could see him for what he is."

"He kills the heathens so that others, Britons, may live without fear. That is not the act of murder but of protection," the young man argued, his voice heating with impatience.

Tanis couldn't let Curran go without knowing the truth. "I speak of Gavin, not some ruddy band of Celts."

"Gavin?"

"Aye, and once upon a time, nearly me."

Curran tilted his head, with a questioning look on his face.

Tanis spread his legs, bracing for the pain he was about to bring upon himself. If exposing one of his deepest secrets to the light for Curran to examine would convince him of the atrocities Luthias committed, then he'd do so willingly. Anything to spare Curran the same fate of Gavin.

"Those scars that fascinated you so. They came from Luthias' own blade."

Curran blanched. "Why? How?"

"It matters not." Tanis turned his back on Curran, his heart so swamped with regrets that he could scarcely breathe. The tentative touch of the younger man's hand on his shoulder brought him back around.

"Everything about you matters to me."

"Liar. We both know you would have sought me out long before now if I appealed to you beyond one night's pleasure." Tanis pulled away from the comfort of Curran's hand. He didn't deserve this man's compassion any more than Luthias did, nor did he want it. "Gavin and I grew up together, entered the Duke's service—Duke Osric, Luthias' father—together, trained together, and..."

"Loved together?" Curran suggested, finding the words Tanis could not bring himself to speak.

"Yes. Until the old Duke discovered us together, in that very pool where we met."

There had been more play involved then. They laughed and made noise, certain their actions would go unnoticed by any human ears. But they had been wrong. So terribly, terribly wrong. And not even sharing a fraction of the Duke's own blood could save them.

"I have heard stories, even in my village, of Osric's fierce temper. Did he punish you for soiling his pool?"

"No, he punished us for a sin he saw as being far greater. That of expressing our love for one another."

"But Gavin ended up a knight. How did that happen if the old Duke thought so little of his value as a man?"

"I never know whether to call it luck or a curse. But as he kept us in chains, ordering Luthias to slice away precious pieces of our hide, Osric died."

Curran shook his head. "I have always heard that Osric died as a result of wounds sustained in battle."

"That was Luthias' doing. With the same blade he'd been using against us, he carved upon Osric's hide before our eyes, a savage attack that seemed to have no reason. Once he returned to his senses, Luthias ordered us to help him deliver the Duke to bed. Since they had not been home long from the most recent campaign, it was a plausible story that any but the family's loyal servants would believe."

"And in gratitude for your assistance, Luthias had a change of heart and spared your life?"

If only the truth were that simple. But Luthias was even better than Osric at binding a man in strings. "Luthias knew he had to kill us or otherwise make it impossible for us to speak out against him. Death, I learned later, he saw as a reward so he came up with a way to keep us alive yet firmly under his thumb. I wanted no part of him or his household, so when asked what menial job I would perform for him, I immediately chose the hunt."

"A job that would take you away from the castle, unable to spread rumors."

"Luthias knew it would take more than absence from the castle walls to hold my tongue. He explained that he would keep Gavin beside him. If I ever broke my silence, Gavin would pay the price with his life as well as I and those I loved most."

Curran paled at the harsh sentence. "Gavin agreed to this?"

"Gavin was given no choice. In my selfishness, I doomed him to be with Luthias until death, his or mine, performing whatever service Luthias saw fit to require."

"But he did not release you from your pledge once he was assured of your good intentions?"

"Once Luthias has you, he will never let you go. Do not fool yourself about this."

There was a silence as Curran mulled over his words. Then he said, "The northern raiders must be stopped before they take my friends and family from their homes, rape their women and steal their property as they have done to so many other villages in the borderlands. So far, the Duke has managed to hold them back, but each year they grow braver and more foolhardy. If Luthias offers me the chance to fight against them, I will stand with him. For that chance, I would pledge my sword to the devil himself."

"You may well be doing just that."

Chapter Eight
~ *Goodbyes* ~

Tanis stirred the bubbling pot with a long stick of wood. The flooring creaked as Curran crossed the room, but he didn't look up. If the young man was determined to throw away his future, his life, on Luthias' whim, there was nothing left to say.

"I did not come here to fight you with, Tanis," Curran said softly.

"Then why did you come?"

"To tell you of my good fortune in case you wondered about my fate, and to..." He trailed off. "Never mind that now. I should go."

"Speak your mind. This may be the only place on the Duke's land where you are free to do so."

Curran seemed to draw courage from those words and laid a hand on his shoulder. "I came to see if you would have me again."

"Luthias would not be pleased if he were to learn of your visit here."

"Be that as it may, tonight I still belong to myself. I want to spend it with you."

Tanis couldn't resist such an appeal, especially when it fit so neatly with his own desires. If this was their last chance to be together, he'd do his best to make it a memorable one.

He spread the burning embers out to cool them then rose to his feet. Curran waited for him, a half smile across his thin, talented lips. He was so beautiful, so full of life. "You are a living dream."

He drew the younger man into his embrace and lowered his lips for a deep kiss. Curran's mouth immediately opened, giving him access to every part. Their tongues met, but rather than a clash of wills they dueled in mutual seduction. Curran melted against him, slipped his arms around Tanis' waist and rubbed his needy, hard cock against Tanis' inner thigh.

This was not destined to be the slow taking Tanis had fantasized about. Their needs were too great, their time together too short.

Tanis guided Curran backward. "My bed."

With a gentle push, Curran tumbled down upon the mattress and spread out with his hands behind his head. His pants pulled tightly across his crotch, showing Tanis how much he enjoyed being there.

Tanis stripped off his shirt first this time, letting the younger man see his scars in the firelight. His boots were tossed somewhere behind him, followed closely by his drawers. The raw evidence of what Luthias was capable of doing to his fellow man was also illuminated by the fire's warm glow.

Curran sat up. He reached out a hand to caress the calloused lines.

"Do they frighten you?" Tanis asked, only then realizing that he had hoped to do just that. Scare Curran into walking away from the Duke, from Otterburn, from him.

"They sadden me." He leaned close to kiss one at the edge of the short, black curls. "I wish you had not been caused such pain."

"It is not pain I feel now," Tanis told him, his voice rough with restrained passion.

The young man kept kissing around the base of his lust. It grew steadily, sometimes brushing against Curran's stubble-roughened cheek as he kept up his light teasing. Then, just as Tanis was reaching the limit of his patience for this kind of play, Curran took his shaft into his mouth.

Tanis gripped a handful of dark blond hair and pulled Curran off his cock. "You have until the count of three to shed your clothes. On four, I shall do it for you and I promise you will have no more than scraps left when I am done."

Curran's eyes widened in surprise as Tanis called out, "One."

Boots and a leather vest hit the floor as Tanis said, "Two."

Tanis let Curran continue to struggle with his tight pants as he uttered, "Three."

Then, like a starving man, he fell upon Curran and ripped his shirt of fine linen in half. He impatiently shoved the fabric aside to get to the well-muscled chest. It looked even better than he remembered. Tasted better too, he discovered as he lowered his mouth to lick Curran's nipple. No water to dilute the man's natural musk.

Curran gasped with pleasure but struggled to gain more freedom of movement. "You are making this task twice as difficult."

Tanis looked down between their bodies where both cocks were freed and rising toward their bellies. "Looks like you are doing a fine job of it to me."

Curran groaned under Tanis' renewed assault of his sensitive nipples but managed to finally kick his legs free of the rugged fabric. Curran planted his heels on the bed and lifted his hips so he could grind against Tanis' belly.

Tanis relished the feel of the hardness rubbing against his skin. He wanted more of that. He wanted more of everything, more of Curran.

He kissed, nipped and licked his way down the younger man's body until he reached Curran's cock. He lightly gripped the rigid shaft between his fingers, and beat his own tongue with the plump head. Curran's eyes rolled back in his head as he attempted to thrust into Tanis' mouth.

Tanis used his weight to anchor Curran's legs, restricting the young man's movement. It had a bonus he hadn't considered, giving him a channel in which to bury his own needy shaft. He rocked his hips in time with his sucking. The soft hair on Curran's legs added to his pleasure until he was in danger of spilling his seed.

Abruptly, he broke away and sat up.

"What is it?" Curran asked, concerned.

"You make me forget myself." He'd been ready to take his lover without so much as a gob of spit to ease the way.

Curran cuddled him from behind. He rested his chin on Tanis' shoulder as his busy hands stroked Tanis' swollen cock. "Tanis."

"What?"

"That is who you are. I like having your name upon my lips as I make love to you."

His heart expanded in the same way the room had contracted earlier. Tanis knew nothing outside the world he and Curran created. A world of passion and emotion and, at least on his side, fear.

"Lard," he said, springing away from the younger man's embrace. "It is all I have but it will do."

"I will never think of it in quite the same way again," Curran replied, laughing.

Tanis located what he sought and brought the container back to the bed. "Top or bottom?"

Curran pierced him to his soul with his pair of clear, sky blue eyes. "I want you inside me, Tanis. Unreservedly, like before."

Tanis swore with wonder as he fell upon his lover. In between slow, drugging kisses, he prepared both of them for entry. Curran tried to turn over but Tanis held him in place.

"Face me this time," Tanis told him. Then seized by a weighty misgiving, he added, "Unless you'd rather not."

The young man reached between their bodies and positioned Tanis' cock right where they both needed it to go. "Now," Curran urged him. "Push. Hard."

It was a tight fit, even better than before. He lifted Curran's legs onto his shoulders so he could drive deeper. He pushed until Curran howled, letting him know he had hit that special spot.

"Do that again," Curran begged him.

Tanis withdrew slightly, then rammed his cock in. Curran bucked under him. He loved the way his balls slapped against Curran's arse. The way the young man tied himself in knots to give Tanis deeper access. The way they fit together, and seemed to share the same needs. It wasn't a matter of deciding who would lead and take their pleasure first; it was mutual need driving them both. Their lust grew together, fueled by their mutual passion.

"Fuck," Tanis growled, his release gathering in his balls. "You make short work of me."

Curran's cock oozed liquid pleasure. He ran his fingers through the pre-come then spread the sticky substance on Tanis' lips. "Maybe this will help. Taste how much I want you to come, Tanis."

Tanis licked off the salty flavor, then drew Curran's fingers inside his mouth. The combination of having something to suck, something to fuck, and the blue-eyed lover who offered him both without reserve undid him. He tilted his head back and let loose a primal roar as he spilled his seed into Curran's tight, sweet arse. He jerked again and again, his climax so strong that it brought black dots to his eyes.

After he shuddered through expelling the last few drops, Tanis lowered himself onto Curran's chest. Arms that had been strengthened through swordplay wrapped around him. The only slight note of discord was the way the young man continued to pant in his ear.

Tanis tried to shift his weight so he was no longer crushing his lover beneath him. Immediately Curran surrounded him with both arms and legs in a firm bear hug. "Do not...move," Curran ordered.

"You need more air," Tanis said, amused that Curran couldn't work that much out for himself.

Then he felt a hard ridge of flesh gliding against his lower belly and realized what Curran's problem really was. And how he could help.

Tanis raised himself on his elbows, putting more pressure on his hips so that Curran's thick cock was pinned between their bodies.

"Oh, God."

"Your turn," Tanis urged him. "Fuck me. Like this."

Curran gripped Tanis' hips and continued the rocking motion. Tanis kept as still as possible, letting Curran use him to maximize his pleasure. The young man's grunts became rhythmic warnings of his impending explosion. Curran's teeth bit into Tanis' shoulder as his body flexed one last time. The sting mattered little in comparison to the way his lover's body tensed and released under him.

When Curran finally opened his eyes and gazed into Tanis', tears shimmered there. Unable to bear seeing them and what they might mean, Tanis rolled away then spooned against the younger man's back. He petted and soothed, the way he would care for any creature in pain. Never before had another man permitted him such intimacy. Curran warmed to it naturally. He was the picture of a sated, content lover and it broke Tanis' much-scarred heart to know he would never see this look on Curran's face again.

Damn Luthias, and the Celts, and the whole bloody world. Damn his bastard of a father, and the choices that had left Tanis impotent to help those he loved most.

Because he had to get out of bed or give in to the urge to keep Curran there forever, Tanis declared the stew ready. They got dressed and ate in silence, pausing frequently to look at each other as if this would be the last occasion they would ever have to do so.

When it came time for Curran to depart, he said, "I will pledge Luthias my sword and my loyalty when he asks for I can do no less and be the man I have been raised to be." He kissed Tanis' cheek where the muscles bunched as he clenched his jaw. "To you, I offer my heart."

Pushed beyond his limits, Tanis growled, "If you intend to offer your life to that monster, I will not have your heart nor any other part of you."

Curran lowered his head in acceptance and pulled away for the final time. "So be it."

Chapter Nine
~ *Forces of Good and Evil* ~

His heavy heart made for heavy tread upon the secret stairs that led from the dungeons to his room and beyond.

He wished he'd had more time with Tanis, to get him to see that serving the Duke was not so bad a fate as he feared. The Duke might be a selfish man, but Curran had never witnessed Luthias commit a truly cruel or unkind act. Surely there was another side to the story Tanis had told about Gavin and his own scars...

Voices carried down the cold tunnel to his ears. At first, Curran assumed it was loud conversation from one of the rooms along the way. However, as he climbed he realized the sound echoed from within, rather than without. He slowed his steps, glad to be wearing soft leather boots that didn't leave a mark of his passing upon the stone.

"Luthias, you motherless cur."

Curran held himself still, even as his breast heaved with the desire to run the traitor through for speaking ill of the Duke.

The Duke's low voice rumbled softly in response. "Let us get on with our exchange, for I like being in your presence no better than you enjoy being in mine, you heathen swine."

The other man spoke with a burr so thick it took Curran an extra moment to puzzle through his meaning. "I'll nae stand for ye to bugger me again, Luthias."

"Refuse me, and your men will die of starvation. Play along, and one or two of them might live."

"What you ask of us, it's nae right."

"The choice is yours, of course. But remember I know where your village lies. It is far more convenient for my troops to travel that short distance than to wage my little war in the land of your enemies."

Although they had paused during this exchange, Curran heard the moment they resumed their descent. He had to hide, or he would be discovered. He took the stairs as quickly and quietly as he could until he reached a door that opened under his hand. He backed inside, and pressed the door closed so that only a crack remained.

Luthias and the other man passed. They carried no lamp in the darkness, as if they'd taken the path so many times they could do it blind. And with no light behind him, Curran couldn't see much of them from his position either. He smelled a hint of horse, saw a flash of plaid, but not enough to confirm if the visitor was a member of a clan that spied for the Duke or one of the enemy raiders who came to barter a truce.

The first seemed more likely. After all, what reason would Luthias have to meet with murdering traitors? It didn't sound as if these two had peace on their mind.

Suddenly a pair of small hands wormed their way under the back of his shirt. Curran stiffened, unsure of where he was or who would be at his back. This wasn't a path he had explored before.

"So it is you, Curran, that he has sent to me tonight. How...unusual."

He knew that voice. It belonged to the Duchess. Not good.

He tried to disentangle her cold, quick hands from his clothing, but she hadn't given him leave to touch her so all he could do was try to move out of her range. "No one sent me, your Grace."

"Always so formal," she said, pursuing him. "You need not keep up that guise here. For once I have been sent a visitor who I will enjoy thoroughly, and there is no need to waste time on formalities."

Again her fingers went to the laces on his shirt. There was no way he wanted to bed her. Even if Tanis hadn't satisfied him so well, it would be impossible for him to rise to the occasion. Her soft body just didn't move him.

"It is no act, your Grace. I speak truly when I tell you I was not asked to come here, but stumbled upon this room by pure happenstance."

Her fingers stilled. "Luthias did not send you to me?"

"No, your Grace. If he had, I would have sought you out in your chamber. How is it that you come to be here?"

His eyes were well adjusted to the darkness, but he could see little in the closed room. No windows for the moonlight to steal in, no candles to bring a soft glow. He thought he could spot a sleeping pallet against the wall, but there was little else in the room. Obviously this room had only one purpose, and the Duchess had somehow been coerced into providing that service.

"Never mind that," she said, nervousness adding a tremor to her voice. "You must leave. Now."

"Would you like me to escort you to your room?" He felt far more comfortable in her presence since she'd retreated of her own accord.

"No. I must remain. Please, get yourself out of here. Forget you ever saw this place, or that we have spoken this night."

It would be easier if she had tasked him with bringing down the moon. There were too many secrets in the castle walls for all to be aboveboard. Evander's words of warning rose to his mind, and he was beginning to believe there was more to his hunch than simply a servant's uneducated fears.

She bumped into him in an effort to shove him out. He moved accordingly, and she glanced through the crack he'd left. "If you hurry, you should make it back to your room before he returns."

"And if I do not?"

"Pray you succeed, young warrior, or not even your brave and honest heart will save you."

⋘⋙

Curran entered his room on catlike feet. He had the strangest urge to check his back for dagger marks.

He stripped to his skin and cleaned up with the cold water left in the washbasin. Thoughts flew through his mind like scattered birds.

What was Luthias' wife doing in that small closet of a room? Who had she been expecting?

Who had the Duke been meeting with, and for what purpose?

Why did the Duchess and Evander demand that he return to his room by a certain hour or suffer dire consequences?

Foolish notions, Curran told himself. Sure, the Duke's conversation seemed a little ominous. Who wouldn't think that after all he'd been told? His mood already black after his disagreement with Tanis, he was much more likely to see the negative aspect of things. In the morning, it would make more sense. He would wait to sort out his impressions then.

Curran climbed into his bed and rested on top of the blankets. Naked, he stretched out, wishing he had been able to spend a few more hours with Tanis instead of having to rush away as he had. But not even those thoughts could keep him awake for long.

He woke an indeterminable amount of time later, while the sky was still painted black. At first he thought nothing of the soft noises, remembering his old barracks where the shifting of other restless bodies was a common occurrence. Then his brain alerted him to his real surroundings, and he sat upright to see who had entered his room.

Four black figures, distinguishable only because their presence blocked out what little light entered through his window, ringed his bed.

"Who the hell are you?" he demanded. "What are you doing in my chamber?"

"Rise and follow," the one to his right intoned.

"I will not. Not until I am given an explanation."

He clutched at the bed linens to cover himself. He was far too exposed without any clothing, any cover, any weapon. His mind spun in a frantic search for options that would allow him to escape or at least warn others that there were intruders inside the castle walls, but no solution presented itself.

The figure to his left tore the heavy blankets from his grasp and dropped them upon the floor.

"Rise and follow," the one on his right repeated.

Seeing he had little choice in the matter, Curran did as asked. "Where are we going? May I dress first?"

"No. Come."

They left by regular means which Curran found more disquieting than if they'd used the secret passages and marched through the castle corridors. He walked behind two of the figures, while the remaining two trailed after him. He thought he knew where they were taking him—to

Luthias' audience chamber—so he was surprised when they stopped before the door to the castle's chapel.

One of the figures opened the door and another one pushed him inside. A fire had been lit in the fireplace behind the table-like altar. Yet despite the warm temperature, Curran shivered. This was no religious ceremony about to take place.

Fat tallow candles sat in braces on the two side walls. Their flames danced gleefully as the group passed, with Curran now in the lead. As they neared the front of the room, the door to the priest's nook opened and Luthias stepped out. The Duke wore a white gown that covered him from shoulder to ankle in much the same way as the black fabric covered the others.

Despite the strange clothing and manner of his arrival, Curran had never been so relieved to see another human being in his life. Surely if he were to be taken into the Duke's household, the man wouldn't let him come to harm.

"Welcome, Curran. You are turning out to be everything I had hoped you would."

Curran bowed his head in acknowledgment of the compliment and bit his tongue against saying that he'd been given little choice in the matter. Being roused from a sound sleep after a disturbing night had been hard on his sunny nature, but it wasn't wise to take his ire out on the Duke.

His escorts fanned out and sat on the first bench, two to either side. Curran was left standing as Luthias ducked into the small storage room at the opposite end of the wall from the Priest's nook. When the Duke returned, he held a chalice in one hand.

"Drink this, and then we will talk."

The fluid in the cup smelled vile. Like rancid honey. He put it to his lips and sipped it under the watchful gaze of the Duke. The stuff tasted worse than it smelled. He held his breath and swallowed the contents in three large gulps.

"Again you exceed my expectations, young Curran. I will have to think of a suitable reward to give Tanis for bringing you to my attention."

"If Tanis had his way, I would not be here at all," Curran admitted, unsure why he felt the need to make sure the Duke knew the truth of it.

"Of that, I have no doubt," Luthias replied. "Still, a favor is a favor and should be rewarded. I will think of something, never fear."

"As you wish, your Grace."

"So willing to please. That is what I like about you, Curran. Your loyalty remains true even when the evidence is contrary to your beliefs."

Curran was distracted from responding by a flare of fire in his belly. He didn't need it as the room was far too warm to begin with. However, he could do nothing to stop the flood of heat that coursed through him, bringing sweat to his brow.

"Do you know why you have been brought here?"

"No, your Grace."

"Because without me you are nothing. You have nothing. Do you understand this?"

Mutely, he nodded. The heat had become a painful burning. He kept his groan inside only because his teeth were clamped so tightly together.

"Speak. Let these witnesses hear your answer."

"Yes, your Grace," Curran panted in between ragged breaths. "I am your loyal, humble servant because without you I am nothing."

White hot pain erupted in his belly and he could no longer hold back a gasp. His legs weakened and, in the next instant, he fell in a heap upon the floor. He curled into a ball, squeezing his eyes shut against the tears that threatened to fall. Curran didn't want to display any sign of weakness in front of the Duke, but he had little control over his own body now.

Dear God, what had he done to deserve such vile treatment?

Curran dimly registered the sounds of the Duke squatting beside him. "Those who serve me must sometimes suffer. Do you have the courage, the strength to accept this without complaint?"

Curran's head bobbed, more from the shudders that wracked his body rather than from any actual agreement on his part.

"Good. You are wise, for those who suffer on my behalf will also know great rewards."

Curran felt several pairs of hands lift him and deposit his body on the long stone slab that served as an altar. The men rubbed his limbs, soothing the cramped muscles. The lip of another cup—this one containing a thick, sweet syrup—slipped between his lips. It coursed down his throat, cooling the burn, and he swallowed automatically.

"See, you now have proof that while being in my service can bring on suffering, I have the power to ease it. This lesson tonight will ensure you remember the full extent of my power."

"I will remember," Curran agreed. Whether or not he said so aloud remained in doubt until the Duke spoke again.

"And will you also remember your pledge to me? That you are mine in mind, spirit and in body?"

"I will."

"Then I welcome you into my innermost circle, Curran Aurick. From this day forth, you will be known as Sir Curran of the House of Otterburn, with all the rights and responsibilities that come with bearing my name. Let all you meet see this sword and know that it is true."

Curran could see the hilt and little else, but that was enough. The pommel contained the Duke's personal crest. He'd finally proven himself and become the knight he'd always dreamed of being. What pain still lingered left his body as he sagged with relief.

He nearly dropped off into the sweet heaven of dreams, but a curious rustling sound had him drawing his lids up one more time. Naked flesh shifted before his eyes. Torsos, buttocks, cocks and shoulders swirled around him.

"What is this?" he asked through lips numb with fatigue.

"Now, Curran, we will share our joy at having you in our ranks."

No way could this be real, Curran thought as he watched the four naked men climb up on the table and straddle his limbs. Each took his own member in hand and stroked it to firmness. The sight was so arousing that Curran felt his own cock harden just by watching them.

"Impressive," Luthias declared, running his finger over Curran's length. "Very few have the reserve to rise to the occasion after drinking of the potions of sin and salvation. I think such strength should be rewarded, don't you?"

Curran couldn't see who the Duke spoke to, but in the next instant the pressure on his thigh changed and he could feel a hot, wet mouth slide over the head of his cock. "Ahhh!"

His back arched as he thrust into that moistness. He felt disconnected from his physical form, almost floating outside of it. The human part of himself that protested this bizarre treatment seemed to be locked away, leaving a base nature in charge of his body. He received the impulses of pleasure but had little control over the way he responded.

The Duke, now equally naked, climbed upon the table as well. He stood over Curran, one foot to either side of his hips and facing him. One of the men changed position to tongue Luthias' balls where they dangled so temptingly. The one sucking Curran's cock increased his pace, drawing him in deeper and with more pressure.

Curran bucked with desire. The Duke closed his eyes and moaned as his knight plied him with the same attentions that Curran was receiving. The two at his shoulders drew closer so they could rub their cockheads together until pre-come glistened from the tips. Curran stuck out his tongue, hoping for a taste, and was rewarded as the pair stroked his tongue with their wetness, fucking his mouth in turns.

Grunts and groans of men approaching the pinnacle of their pleasure filled the chamber. So overwhelmed with the need for release, Curran couldn't even give his partner a warning as his seed spilled out in a mighty river. As if that were the signal to the rest, one by one the men came. The Duke held out the longest, waiting until all eyes were on him. His gaze locked on Curran, mouthing the word *Mine* over and over as he spilled his semen upon Curran's chest.

Curran either fell asleep or, more likely, blacked out then. He faded in and out as he was carried back to his room. Evander was there, waiting for him. The men left as silently as they had arrived. The servant ignored them, already tending to Curran's needs. He wiped the sticky mess from his skin, all the while muttering about immoral wickedness and evils of the flesh.

Then another fragment of time vanished and Curran found he was alone. He rolled over, punched his pillow, and determined that the surreal interlude had been nothing more than a twisted dream, perhaps brought on by a bit of tainted meat combined with his lingering desire for Tanis.

Until his hand drifted to the other side of the bed where it encountered the steel reminder of oaths made and promises given.

Chapter Ten
~ *Defeat* ~

The following morning, Curran was roused by the sounds of movement nearby. Persistent and painful when the noise crashed into the fragile material left between his ears, Curran ducked under his pillow to hide.

"None of that, Sir Curran. You have to be up and about, or you will be left behind on your first campaign."

"Stop shouting," Curran ordered, his head in danger of breaking, like a tree that bursts when its sap freezes from the cold. His head had never ached so bad. Worse than any hangover he'd ever known.

And what was the "sir" business?

The servant stomped over to the bed, removed the pillow. "Up and about."

"You cruel beast. Do you get joy from causing pain to others?" Curran sat up. That process brought so much nausea he couldn't force himself to march on with the next step, that of opening his eyes.

"It is not my heart that gives shelter to the evil in this place," Evander replied, finally using a tone that was just a hair lower than mind-splitting.

The servant brought a large pitcher to the bed. Curran was about to take back some of the nasty things he said to the angel of mercy who brought him water to chase away the furry beast nesting in his mouth. Then the little toad of a man upended the pitcher of cold water over Curran's head, shocking his system into wakefulness whether it welcomed the change or not.

"The Duke plans to leave in an hour. Get dressed and meet him in the courtyard. His Grace expects you to ride at his side."

That news brought a joyous leap to Curran's heart. Whatever happened the night before, what little he remembered no longer worried his conscience. It was a one-time ordeal, a rite of passage. Surely things would be different now.

CB80

As it turned out, things were different once they left Duke Luthias' lands, but not necessarily better. Curran soon realized the Duke wasn't as well-equipped as he had thought to lead his men into battle. All the noble qualities a strong leader should possess deserted Luthias when it came time to make war. The Duke's confidence overrode all other considerations. He expected to win easily. The details were unimportant to him, and their ability to wage effective war suffered for it.

Curran circulated through the men each night, listening to their chatter and doing what he could to rectify their complaints. Luthias disliked having his favorite knight disappear for hours at a time. He preferred to keep his innermost circle around him, like acolytes at his altar. In the end, Curran was forced to forgo sleep to make sure that all the loathsome details the Duke relegated to low-ranking, clueless officers were getting done in proper fashion.

He blamed this lack of rest for failing to recognize the Celts were setting a trap until it was too late to extract the Duke's men. The heathens lured the Duke's troops into the hills, their home ground. Luthias pursued them, unwilling to end the chase now that his quarry was on the run.

Through the dense trees, the Duke pressed on. His fighters lost their advantage when the underbrush snarled around their limbs. Without the freedom to maneuver, they were sitting ducks when the rain of Celtic arrows came down.

Luthias had provided swords for his recruits, but given the number of new ranks there hadn't been time to produce body armor or give them much training. The small shields they hid behind did little to prevent them from taking an arrow in the knee. Or the face.

As God protects imbeciles and children, so he protected Luthias' army that day. The arrows quickly dried up, giving Curran a chance to order his charges to withdraw, out of weapon range.

The Duke ordered the men to rally for another charge up the hill. Thankfully, the horn he used to convey such commands was one of the casualties of the melee. Curran pretended not to hear the faint call over the breaking of sticks and groans of the injured men as the survivors carried their wounded brothers back to the relative safety of their camp.

The trip back was far shorter than the march out. Nothing stood in their way, and they didn't have to fight for every inch of bloody ground they covered.

Blood of their own men.

Blood that didn't have to be shed.

Blood, Curran vowed, that wouldn't go to waste.

There was a lesson to be learned here, and he would make damn sure Luthias learned it as well as he.

Curran didn't have time to rehearse his speech. When he followed Luthias into the tent the knights used as their barracks, he spoke plainly. "Your Grace, what plans have you to return to the castle?"

"Return?" The Duke handed his helmet over to a waiting servant. "I plan to return to the battlefield, not the castle."

"We lost a third of our men today. We need more time to prepare a plan of attack that will yield better results than this."

More men from the Duke's inner circle joined them, and began to strip the armor from Luthias' body. "I agree our methods must be altered to meet this new challenge, young Curran. Our enemy has grown bolder over the last few encounters."

"They have grown smarter as well," a grizzled veteran added.

Curran noticed the way the grim-faced warrior kept his sword within arm's reach at all times, as Curran did. The Duke had handed his blade over to a servant. Had the man learned nothing from his experiences these past years? Attacks could come at any time, without warning. This wasn't a holiday or a job where the sword could be hung up for the night like a cook's ladle.

"Perhaps," Luthias admitted. "Even the stupidest of animals can be taught a new trick."

"You think one of our men is teaching them how to counter our English tactics?" one of the knights asked the Duke.

Anger flashed across Luthias' face. "No. No one would dare defy me that way."

Curran balanced on the balls of his feet, bursting with desire to fling himself at the Duke and shake some sense into him. "Perhaps we could discuss the day's events, see what we can learn from them."

Now dressed in a loose robe, Luthias sat upon a scaled-down version of his throne. "Ah, young Curran, you have a warrior's heart but you do not appreciate the benefits of victory. Half the joy to be found in waging war is the way we divide our enemy's spoils at the end of the day."

Several of the knights who milled about the large tent laughed at this response. Only the veteran seemed to sense Curran's seriousness and the reasons behind it. Did they not understand what had happened in those hills? "Your Grace, it is not the spoils that need our attention this night, but rather the battle itself. We must speak of the mistakes made today so that we may not repeat them on the morrow."

Luthias' eyes narrowed. "Mistakes? I think you are confused, boy. We won. Our enemy was forced into retreat."

"Only because the Celts ran out of arrows."

Luthias shook his head. "So disappointing, I agree. I, too, wish for a more challenging opponent. It hardly seems worth getting out of bed to face them. Perhaps if we are more aggressive, they will put up a better fight."

Curran couldn't help himself. He choked over that. "More aggressive? That rash attack, following those men on land where they have spent generations, cost us nearly a third of our men. Do you not see that lives are being needlessly spent by your reckless tactics?"

Light noise, that of men gorging on drink and shedding their tools of war, suddenly turned to silence. Luthias sat up straighter in his chair, staring at Curran with cool blue eyes. "What I see is a careless man on the verge of committing treason."

Curran sucked in a breath and let it out slowly. As he did, he bowed deeply. "I beg your forgiveness, your Grace. I meant no offense."

The Duke waved his hand dismissively. "I forget that you have not fought with us before. It is natural that you feel some disquiet the first time blood is spilled by your own blade." Luthias raised his hand, then clenched his fingers with a dramatic flair. "In time, you will grow to love the power of holding a life on the tip of your sword. To set it free or snuff it out on your whim."

The Duke's passionate tone turned Curran's blood to ice. The scales fell away from his eyes, and he looked upon Luthias with true vision. For the first time, he saw the monster inside the man, the very real evil that Evander had spoken of. It sapped the strength from his knees. He crashed to the floor. To God, he said, "I do not understand."

However, it was the Duke who answered him. "You will, in time," he assured Curran. "Rest now. We will speak more of this after we have feasted."

The men went back to their drinking. Activity swirled around Curran as his brain wrestled with this new, terrifying discovery. Luthias wasn't a noble, seeking to protect his kingdom from marauders. He thought of them as dogs, taunting them into attack so he could punish them for their disobedience. He was a bully. All the songs of praise about his battle prowess were nothing more than wind to further inflate his gigantic ego.

One of the knights brushed against him. Wine spilled down the back of his neck. It shook Curran out of his stupor, giving him the motivation to move. He got to his feet, his legs still unsteady, and started toward the flap that would take him out of this strange nightmare and into the moon's healing glow.

An arm encased in steel blocked his path. Curran glanced at the man who had doused him. His eyes reflected more sobriety than his clumsy nature would have one believe. "Let me pass," Curran muttered softly.

The battle-hardened knight steered Curran toward the back of the tent, away from the Duke and his companions. "Let your tongue loose like that again, and you will not live to see the dawn."

"I do not deserve to." He'd done nothing, *nothing*, to protect the innocent from Luthias' rampage. No wonder the heathens raided their lands if this was the kind of treatment they were accustomed to from the British nobles. To be hunted like wild animals for sport...it was hardly the act of a virtuous Duke. And by association, the blame trickled down to all those who fought in his name.

The veteran gave Curran's shoulder a hard shake. "Be sensible, boy. What good will you do anyone if you are short a head?"

"Without honor, a man is nothing."

"He is alive. I would say that is a damn sight better than not."

How could Curran make the man understand? He'd rather be dead than follow the Duke into another senseless, brutal confrontation. "I cannot kill for sport. I cannot kill for a man who treats his subjects like pawns on a chessboard."

"Too late for that. You accepted Luthias' offer of family and friendship. You carry his sword on your hip, and his favor on your arm. Kill or be killed. Those are your choices now. Be quick to know your heart and mind. Luthias will not allow you much time to decide, and his brand of justice is often brutal."

Curran left the tent and walked among the wounded. He had no words to brighten their sagging spirits. This was not the way things were supposed to be.

And yet, how could they be any different? Luthias would not change. Curran didn't waste a moment trying to fool himself into believing otherwise. He'd already lost too much to false dreams. But what options did that leave him? Even if he chose the life of a vagabond, the shame of breaking his word, of putting his life above his vows, would kill him more quickly than an arrow through his head. At least by staying there was a chance he could save another innocent pawn from death, even if it was far too little, far too late.

He arrived at this answer as dusk closed the curtain on day. The knights would be feasting on whatever rations Luthias ordered. Curran had no appetite, and no desire to return to the Duke's side. He was about to find a quiet spot in which to lie down when a runner approached him at top speed, falling against Curran, out of breath.

"Sir Knight, his Grace wishes to see you at once."

"Tell him I have had too much entertainment this day and must retire."

"Duke Luthias said more blood will be spilled if you do not," the lad said in between pants.

Curran didn't question whose blood that would be. It didn't matter. As the old warrior had said, Luthias would not willingly give up his entertainment.

With a determined stride to beat the Duke at whatever game he was playing now, Curran went where summoned. "You wished to see me, your Grace," he said upon entering the Duke's presence.

Candles now flickered from their holders to either side of Luthias' chair. The remains of a meal littered the wooden table set in the center of the lavish tent. One plate was left untouched. His own. Flies now buzzed around it, feasting on the dead meat.

There was one other addition to the setting, that of a young woman. Long hair covered her face, but not even the layer of mud caked on her body could throw her gender into doubt. She wore a leash fashioned from long strips of leather and nothing more. Although her position was supposed to imply subservience, her expression remained defiant.

As Curran came forward, the woman tried to bolt. Although Luthias' attention was no longer on her, he remained attentive of her position. A quick yank of the leash brought her back to his side.

"Worse than a dog," Luthias said, disgusted. "This one is all teeth and no brain."

"If she does not make a good pet, then perhaps you should return her to the wild. An inferior creature would not survive long there." For a second, Curran thought his suggestion had worked to gain the woman's freedom, but Luthias disappointed him with his next breath.

"Wounded animals can howl for days before they die. So depressing. I would not want to subject our men to that." He turned his head to look at his loyal knights. "Which among you would like to put this creature out of her misery?"

Several men stepped forward, including—to Curran's amazement—the old warrior. How could he be so callous? Did no one else but him see how wrong this was?

Luthias smiled upon the men who offered. "You are good-hearted to spare me the trouble, but I think it is time young Curran learned what power there is in death."

His anger generated a flush of heat that he couldn't quell. "No."

"Are you defying me?" Luthias asked, a faint frown upon his lips.

Yes, I will never be party to this kind of brutality, his heart screamed even as his lips said, "This is not needful."

"Fear of the unknown holds you back, Curran, not these morals you cling to. I knew the day I saw you with the hunt master that you share the same dark desires I possess. I promise once you do this for me, you will understand why it is necessary."

Dark desires? What he had shared that night with Tanis was bright and warm. There was no shame in it.

117

Unorthodox to many, perhaps, but not morally wrong. Taking a life that did not threaten his own was wrong in every way. "Your Grace, I cannot do as you ask."

"I am not asking." Luthias' voice became cold and soft. "Death, once promised a soul, will claim his due. Your life or hers, Curran. Which will it be?"

Chapter Eleven
~ *More Blood Spilled* ~

"Mine then," Curran replied without hesitation. Until death was his vow to Luthias. He'd sworn to do no harm to the Duke, to defend him in all things. That left only himself. To take his own life would be a sin, but perhaps sacrificing himself to save another would buy back enough of his darkened soul to send him to Heaven.

The woman looked at him with eyes full of confusion.

"Ah, so wise of you, Curran. I would be saddened to lose my newest warrior so soon and for such a petty reason."

Before Curran could stop him, before he had a chance to explain that he was willing to sacrifice his life so that she might keep hers, and not the other way around as Luthias obviously assumed, Luthias snapped the woman's neck. Her body fell to the floor at his feet.

"Even in death she is a bother," the Duke said, kicking her corpse away with the toe of his boot. "Curran, dispose of this trash, will you?"

Nausea clogged his throat. He swallowed several times before he could speak, and even then he barely recognized the harsh, raspy voice as his own. "I cannot. I will not."

Luthias sighed heavily. "All this arguing has made me weary, Curran. Do not seek to test me further, or you will find that I am no longer in a forgiving mood."

"Someone must get you to see reason, your Grace. I swore to protect you and I see now that the greatest danger you face is from your own misguided heart."

The Duke's face purpled with rage. "You go too far."

"I have not gone far enough—" A heavy blow landed on the back of his head. Whether it was flesh or wood or steel, it delivered a shock that froze his limbs. He toppled over on his back, his eyes open, blinking from the pain. The rest of him was unable to move.

Luthias stood over him. "Curran, you disappoint me. I thought I had gotten to you in time, but I see now that you are far too flawed to be the type of man I need. I hereby release you from your vow."

The Duke bowed low. When he straightened, he drew Curran's sword from its sheath in a slow hiss. His wrist spun the blade. Curran could feel the sting where the sharp steel nipped his flesh as it slashed away his clothes.

"Before me, you were nothing. I shall return you to the world in the same fashion." Luthias jabbed the sword in the direction of one of his men. "Chain him up with the prisoners. He will travel to the castle with them where he can then be held in the dungeon until he can be tried for treason."

ભ્ર૬૦૬૪

The other prisoners did little to help him on the long trek back to the Duke's castle. Curran didn't blame them at all. He'd been partly responsible for their capture, and was glad they confined their ire to stealing his meager rations rather than his life. However, walking the considerable distance was a lot harder than riding. Without food or decent clothing, the winter was as much his enemy as the people around him. More than once he stumbled to the ground. He struggled to his feet and marched on because he had to, but there was little energy left over for thought.

Home. Tanis. Help. Love. The words swam through his consciousness as he put one weary, bloody foot in front of the other. They became a litany that made it possible to take the next step, and the next and the next. He drew strength from them, praying he would live long enough to see that those things he cherished most were kept safe from Luthias' wrath.

He could no longer name the day—so many had passed in the same numb blur—when they arrived at the castle. True to his word, Luthias had him thrown into one of the dark, damp cells that he'd found during his nighttime sojourns. Unlike the soldiers, the men who guarded him here were his friends. While they couldn't free him, they did see to it that he got his fair share of the rations and that no one harmed him unduly.

During the long dark nights, he lay in a corner, curled up to conserve his body heat. The low murmurs of the other prisoners washed over him like a babbling brook. He paid them no attention, so lost in his own misery that he couldn't spare a thought or a care for those trapped with him. There was a burning in his gut that wouldn't go away, and he feared some of his toes had been lost to frostbite. A swordsman without his toes—his balance—was as good as dead. He couldn't possibly be of use to anyone in that condition, let alone be capable of single-handedly putting a stop to the Duke's butchery.

Evander had been right to warn him. An evil did dwell in these stone walls. Knavish and cold, night after night, he could feel it creeping into his bones. It was evil, straight from hell's own fires. Eating away at his life, his soul. No doubt it corrupted anyone who lived within its reach for long. Luthias was consumed by it. Certainly many others in his inner circle were too.

But not him.

He'd almost been lost. Almost.

Had he not met the gentle hunt master first, he might have been completely fooled by the Duke's many charms. But having Tanis show him those scars—dear Lord, what the man had been made to suffer!—did more than any warning from a servant could. The man most deserving of his allegiance and unconditional love wasn't the one who wore the crown, but rather the quiet man living in the woods alone. The one who tended to sick birds and only killed for food. Well, Tanis had his love now, for all the good it did either of them...

Tanis...

Hearing his lover's name on another man's lips jerked him out of his reverie. His abrupt movement cut off their conversation. Adjusting his position, as if he were just restless rather than alert, seemed to reassure them and they resumed their conversation.

"'Tis the hunt master we want..."

"...not easy..."

"...by force if necessary."

"...must obey the The Lowlander."

Their harsh speech was difficult for Curran to understand. He'd had little practice interpreting it. However, it seemed clear that these prisoners were part of a plot to kidnap Tanis. Did this Lowlander seek to make an exchange of prisoners—Tanis for the lives of those taken during battle? Luthias would agree to no such thing. It could only end badly for Tanis. Tanis, who had done nothing to deserve this. Tanis, who healed, not harmed. Tanis, his beloved.

Curran knew his life was forfeit now anyway. He could sit here in the cell and wait for death to claim him, or he could make one more attempt to redeem himself by warning Tanis of the danger headed his way.

But in order to do that, he had to escape.

This castle was his home. He knew its secrets better than most. He'd find a way out.

He sorted through his options, examining each of them closely. It took several hours; he noticed their passing only by the changing of the guard. How could he leave without the other prisoners making a fuss? How many poor victims could he manage to take with him? He had little strength left. Would it be enough?

By dawn he had a plan. Night returned before he had a chance to carry it out. Sooner or later the Duke would summon some of the prisoners to his audience chamber. Not the public one, but rather, he suspected, the one in which the strange fealty oath had taken place. Curran's heart broke for the souls Luthias would torture and torment. Perhaps by sparing a few of them, he could make up for some of the blights now staining his own immortal spirit.

He took his chance when the guards left their post to escort a small group of prisoners away. Escaping the cell was a simple matter. He knew the key was rarely extracted from the other side of the door, thus decreasing the chances of it being lost or accidentally removed from the dungeon by one of the many guards. Besides, stepping out of the cell would normally put them in the hands of the enemy so there was little point in attempting to escape. Curran, however, had an advantage that most who ended up in these cells didn't. He knew exactly where he was going and how to get there.

Using straw he braided together to form a miniature noose, Curran managed to unlock the door. Rough hands grabbed at him and he hissed at them to back off. Though they might not have understood his words, they did get his meaning. He held up three fingers. He thought three he could safely smuggle out with him.

He didn't delay to see who they'd send. He slipped through the door and checked the stairs leading up to the secret chambers he'd found hidden in the foundation walls. No noise echoed back to him so he took an extra second to secure a small knife better suited to cutting steak than slaying a foe from the table where the guardsmen on duty would sit and play cards. When he looked back over his shoulder, he saw an old man standing in the cell's entrance with one hand on the shoulder of each young child in front of him. The girls were no more than ten. Fear brightened their dark eyes even in the dim light.

Curran cursed under his breath. He'd expected warriors who knew how to move quickly and quietly, not a grandfather and pair of young kids. Still, there was no time to argue. The next part was the most dangerous. If they didn't leave the stairwell before someone came to check on them, they'd surely be caught.

He nodded once, then laid a finger over his lips. He got no response from the small group so he turned his back to them, hoping they would simply follow his lead.

The old man shoved the girls ahead of him, putting them between Curran and himself. He could feel their small bodies crowd against his back as he started down the stairs. As if reliving a memory, his body naturally followed the quietest route, sticking to the curve of the wall and avoiding the places that were too loose to bear his weight without protest. He kept one ear open to the sounds below, another listened to the footsteps of those behind him. They were surprisingly adept at matching his moves, but he didn't dare to believe they were actually going to make it out unscathed until he reached the door at the end of a short hall.

For one long moment, Curran hesitated. It all seemed too easy. The escape from their cell, their flight down the stairs... What if Luthias and his men were playing a game of cat and mouse? What if they lay in wait on the other side of the door?

One small hand grazed his wrist. Though it was too dark to see her face, Curran felt the question in that tentative touch. Right. What *was* he waiting for? Their chances were no better if they attempted to return to the cell. Might as well press on, no matter what awaited them.

The latch was hidden in the frame of the door. Curran's experienced fingers found it after a few seconds of searching. He planned on opening it slowly, but the smaller of the two girls pushed past him opening it wide. He jumped after her, a knife in his free hand. The darkness was absolute except where the light from the torches high on the castle wall cast flickering shadows on the wet, heavy snow.

The girl hadn't gotten far, bolting into the deepest bank. Curran caught her in two strides and jerked her backward against him. She fought him like a demon. It took far more of his meager reserves than he would have liked to restrain her.

He scrambled back against the exterior wall of the castle. To his surprise, the old man had shut the door and waited with the other girl tightly in his grasp. The girls reached for each other, and Curran let his burden go. It was far easier to concentrate on surviving without having to worry about being kicked in the shins. He fought to slow his breathing so he could listen for signs of stirring over the rushing of blood through his veins.

There was definitely someone moving along the castle ramparts. There could be any number of innocent explanations for that, so Curran didn't panic. Yet. But he did gesture to the grandfather that they had unwanted company.

The old Celt gave him a short nod, seemingly content to follow Curran's lead a little while longer. The only thing they could do really was wait. To walk even the short distance from the fortress to the woods would mean crossing through the moonlight. They'd be totally exposed to anyone looking down from the ramparts. Better to wait where they couldn't be easily seen until the guard moved on.

Long seconds passed. Cold from the deep snow seeped into his boots. They barely qualified as such now, being more like rags than the fine leather they'd once been. His feet quickly turned numb, which was both a blessing and a curse. He tried to shut out such thoughts and concentrated on his goal, that of reaching Tanis to warn him.

Finally he decided that they'd given the guard enough time to move on. There were no more noises from above, and no bulky shadows disturbed the light playing over the ground in front of them. They'd have to make one mad dash for the trees, then part ways and hope the falling snow would hide their tracks before someone else stumbled across them.

Again he communicated with hand signals. He counted down, five...four...three...

"Noooooo!"

The feminine wail startled him. The male chuckles that followed didn't do much good for his strained nerves either.

Sounds of a struggle ensued, and from the harsh comments being made it was clear the woman was being towed along against her will. There was very little ceremony to the process, and Curran feared the worst was about to happen.

He didn't have long to wait for confirmation.

She fell to the ground in a graceful arc, almost as if she were flying. The impact of her body hitting the snow made little sound. Next to him, the old Highlander had his arms wrapped around the girls, holding them tightly against his chest. His eyes blazed with a thirst for revenge.

Curran could relate. *That's two I owe you, Luthias, you black-hearted bastard.*

The soldiers' footsteps retreated. Instinct more than any detectable signal kept him still. Once again, it saved his life for a lingering man pissed out into the night, raining his disdain on the broken corpse below. A soft chuckle followed it before he hastened away.

Curran curled his hands into fists and fought back tears of rage that would obscure his sight. He didn't have to get closer to the woman to know it was one of those they'd taken upstairs shortly before he escaped. They'd made her march all this way, and for what? To toss her over the parapet as if she held no more value than the contents of a chamber pot.

It took several deep, calming breaths to suppress his urge to go tearing through the castle on a murdering rampage. He had to remind himself that he'd once been proud to be counted among those guards, and that not all of them were as morally bereft as Luthias. He wouldn't let his anger turn him into the type of man the Duke had become.

Besides, he had a mission and it didn't involve spilling blood.

He gave a curt nod to the old warrior then stepped out into the moonlight. He felt as though he had a target painted on his back. He'd be dead in seconds if the guards spotted him. His tracks would be suspicious, but he didn't dare waste even more time by skirting around the edges of the large field. There was precious little cover there anyway, and no doubt the alarm would soon be raised when they found out he—and perhaps the others— was missing.

He ran as fast as his numb legs would carry him, falling time and time again only to push himself upright once more and soldier on. He never looked back to see where the man and his charges had gone. They were on their own now, and they had a much better chance at survival than their fellow villagers. He'd given them that much, he could do no more.

No, the only one Curran could see to now was Tanis. Tanis of the dark hair and well-muscled back. Tanis with the gruff exterior that hid his heart of gold. Tanis, his love.

He could only pray to a God that he was no longer certain he believed in that he'd reach the hunt master before the Celts did.

But the trip seemed much longer than it should have. The night closed in around him. A blanket of snow changed the shape of the landscape until he was no longer certain of his whereabouts. He could only do his best to find his way despite his confusion and hope that by some twist of fate he'd end up where he most needed to be.

That was his last clear thought before he lost his footing and sprawled face first into the snow. This time when he fell, he didn't have the strength to rise. He pushed, willing his numb limbs to respond, but they seemed much heavier than they should. Far too heavy for him to lift. In fact, the mere effort was starting to make him warm and sleepy...

He let out a defeated sigh and surrendered to the forces of nature that had finally overwhelmed him.

Chapter Twelve
~ *Between the Worlds* ~

No news.

For a bunch of gossiping old hags, it seemed remarkable that no one in the local taverns had word of the Duke's return. Oh, that he was again in residence was agreed upon throughout the surrounding territory. That he'd brought prisoners with him was also widely accepted as fact. But what of the men who rode with him?

Nothing. Not so much as a melodious note or a dry verse.

"Curran, where are ye?" Tanis asked aloud.

The night gave him no answers. Not even Athena had a shrill note for him.

Suddenly it occurred to Tanis that there might be another reason the forest was quiet. *Predators.*

He freed his hunting knife from its sheath. The moonlight couldn't penetrate much of the thick foliage to cast a gleam upon the blade. He held it against his thigh as he listened for signs that he wasn't alone.

There. A soft rustling that didn't come from any breeze. Big for an animal, small for a man.

He crept closer to the underbrush. His quarry maintained the lead, using the darkness as a cloak. Smart critter, whatever it was.

Tanis followed the sounds of movement through the snow-choked forest. They were getting near the river that divided Luthias' lands in half. No doubt he'd be able to spy the creature when it attempted to cross the shallow water.

But when he broke out of the woods, the first thing he noticed was the form of a fallen man, a man of a beggar's station with rags wrapped around his feet and horrible rents in his thin clothes, laying with his feet in the stream that had yet to ice over. Could this be the predator he'd been after? Tanis thought not. The body was too still to have been fleeing before him so adeptly just moments before.

He approached the prone figure and nudged his ribs with the toe of his boot. Not so much as a wisp of air escaped the prone man's lips. He prodded again, this time a little harder. Hard enough to roll the man onto his back.

The moonlight fell upon his face, and Tanis gasped. Curran.

For the time it took to blink, Tanis was amused by the way his young man seemed drawn to bodies of water. But even as the ghost of a smile curled his lips, Tanis dropped to his knees beside his lover. His hunting knife fell to the snow, forgotten as he gripped Curran by the shoulders and gave him a gentle shake. "Curran. Curran!"

There was no response, not from the still man nor from the surrounding hills. He felt a gaze upon his back, one not too friendly. It made the spot between his shoulders itch for thick steel plating, but he remained rooted to his exposed position at Curran's side. With trembling fingers, he reached out to search for even the faintest sign that all was not lost.

"He lives," a rough voice assured him.

Tanis spun around on his knees to face the short man who had confronted him. "Who are you to say?"

The speaker broke from the line of trees and came forward, hands raised in a gesture of peace. He was old, his face creased by the turning of many, many seasons. He wore the garb of a Celt, but didn't seem to have trouble understanding English. "My name is not important. Only life matters here."

Curran made a noise that approximated agreement. Tanis wanted to weep with joy, but he wasn't about to turn his back on this stranger. "Do you refer to the taking of one? Or the giving?"

"That is now for you to decide." The old man nodded, then turned to go.

Tanis waited until the man had disappeared into the trees. He glanced around to be sure he was alone with Curran once more, then again he reached out, brushed the long hair aside to feel for the pulse of life against Curran's neck.

Against all odds, it was there. Faint, yet steady.

"Curran," Tanis said softly. "It is time I take you home."

"No!"

The word was surprising for its suddenness as well as its vehemence. Surely Curran didn't think he would come to harm in his care. Was he in some fever dream, unable to tell friend from foe? "It is I, Tanis. Open your eyes and know me."

The lids fluttered and eventually rose. His blue eyes were filled with pain but slowly focused on him. "Tanis?"

"Yes, love. I am here."

His eyes grew wide with terror. "No, no. You must leave. Leave before he finds you!"

"Calm yourself, Curran. No harm will come to me. It is you who is in danger. Now lie still, and let me pull you from the water."

The movement proved to be too much for the injured man, and he slipped into the unnatural sleep of one who was gravely ill.

Tanis cast out a slew of promises to whatever deity might be listening. Whatever the price, he'd gladly pay it if only Curran survived. Not knowing whether Curran lived or died under the command of Luthias had nearly killed him these last few weeks. Though he might have lost all chance at having Curran's friendship, let alone his love, Tanis vowed to spend each remaining day doing whatever made Curran's heart most glad. Even if it meant biting his tongue about Luthias' treachery to do it.

Tanis constructed a litter by lashing branches together with dead grasses he braided into rope. The deep cold made his fingers clumsy, but he managed the task with the ease of long practice. Getting Curran's body to lie upon it, however, took some doing. The young man groaned with each shift, but Tanis knew the pain would get worse before it got better.

The trek home was long and slow going, and it was nearly dawn by the time they reached it. Athena waited for him there with a dead, fat rabbit on the ground in front of his door. "You're a sweet lass, Athena. That will make a fine stew to heal our wounded friend."

She made a sound more appropriate to a lovesick dove rather than the fierce hunter she was. She then took flight and Tanis brought his lover inside.

From that day on, Tanis remained at home. Since he'd received no official word of the Duke's return, he didn't feel obligated to freeze his hide tracking game in the snow. He had plenty of grain and salted meat stored up to feed him and Curran, so he chose instead to watch over his lover.

Keeping him clean and fed—when he was awake enough to swallow—quickly fell into a routine. Tanis didn't mind a bit. It gave him time to think about what he'd say when Curran was well enough to listen. The fact that the man curled against his warmth whenever he was near made Tanis feel both humbled and strong. He hoped that meant Curran wasn't as angry as his confused words at the stream had seemed.

Their solitude couldn't last forever though. If nothing else the kitchen would soon send down a servant with an order for more meat. Therefore, he wasn't surprised when late one night there was a knock at the door.

Tanis roused himself from the pallet on the floor and crossed the room. With one mighty jerk, he opened the portal and spotted Luthias' personal servant, Evander.

His would-be guest stammered, "Greetings, hunt master. I come with orders from the Duke."

"For food? What'll it be then?"

The servant restlessly moved his feet. Tanis thought it was more from fear than from the cold.

"No, it is not meat that His Grace is wanting."

Tanis could think of only one other item Luthias would come to him for, and there was no way in hell Tanis was going to let the twisted man get his hands on Curran again, at least not until Curran woke and made his own wishes clear. "Have your say, then, and be gone."

"Duke Luthias has learned that Sir Curran yet lives despite being kidnapped from his home by the northern savages. I am to take him back to the castle where he will be well tended."

Tanis glared down at the small man. "Not as long as there is breath within me."

"I am permitted to extend an invitation to you as well, should you be wanting to stay by Sir Curran's side."

That was a twist Tanis hadn't expected. Luthias hadn't allowed him further than the kitchens since the night he'd become Master of the Hunt. What was the sneaky, spineless bastard up to now?

Whatever it was, Tanis needed time to think. He retreated to the corner where Curran shifted restlessly, lost in the shadow world of dreams. Evander took the open door as an invitation and stepped into the dim cabin. He shut the door behind him, grunting with the effort.

After settling the blankets over his lover once more, Tanis fished out a tankard from the pile of dirty dishes, cleaned it with the tail of his shirt, then filled it with mead. He didn't offer any to his guest. "What are you about, Evander?"

"No tricks, hunt master. I would not risk turning His Grace's ire upon me by doing other than what he has asked."

Tanis suspected the old servant spoke the truth in that respect at least. "Why wait until now to summon Curran to the castle? He's been with me for nearly a fortnight now."

"I was not given such information to share with you, hunt master."

The fire would soon require more wood, Tanis observed as he rested his arm upon the warm stone mantle. He sipped from his cup before he replied, "Well, then, I believe there is only one answer I can give you to take to Luthias. No."

"I pray you, reconsider."

"Why should I? I can provide everything Curran needs to heal here in this shelter. There is no reason to move him. In fact, it could be quite dangerous to do so as he continues to stand on the bridge between this world and the next."

"It is not only his life that hangs in the balance," Evander said, his voice taut with nerves.

"Explain yourself."

"You know of the monster the Duke has become. If you choose not to take up this offer, it will be all the worse for those who lack your freedom."

"Speak sense, man. Luthias is cruel, but his love of pageantry would not let him behave in a manner less than kingly in front of his own subjects."

"There was a time when I would have agreed with you. That time has passed."

"What will he do if I refuse? Has he made threats?"

The servant shook his head. "No threats are necessary. Those who dwell inside the keep know well the evil that walks the halls."

"You have been spending far too much time with the old maids in the kitchen, Evander. I admit Luthias has a dark side, but he craves power, not death." Tanis took another long drink from his cup, then set it down. "You have my answer. Curran and I will remain here."

Sad eyes returned Tanis' gaze. "Then keep your doors locked and your knives sharp, hunt master, for this evil has a very long reach."

Chapter Thirteen
~ *Healing* ~

Staying away from the castle's dark halls wasn't an option for long. The northern raiders had mounted an attack against the Duke, sweeping across his lands like a plague of insects, devouring or confiscating everything in sight on their direct march to Luthias' stronghold.

Tanis heard the dire warnings whenever he visited the castle kitchens. Was it best to huddle in his cottage with a sick man and hope the conquering hordes would ignore him? Fat chance. They had no reason to show him mercy and who knew what torture they had in mind for one of the Duke's favorite warriors? No, they'd have to retreat inside the castle walls...eventually.

He put off the move as long as possible. Curran spent most of the time in fevered dreams, talking nonsense about plots and spies and danger. He only quieted when he felt Tanis' arms around him, his soothing rumble murmuring in his ear. Inside the castle walls they'd be under Luthias' constant gaze and subject to his whims. Tanis hated the necessity, but even more he'd hate to lose Curran's life to the same fiends who had murdered Gavin.

The next time Evander came knocking, Tanis consented to go with him. There was little time to spare, so Tanis took only the medicines he'd collected to treat Curran's ailments and what hunting supplies he could spare, and then set out for the Duke's home with Curran cradled against his chest.

Unexpectedly, Luthias had ordered that they be given a room in the tower... Gavin's old room. Tanis saw immediately that this had been Curran's living quarters long enough to meld his belongings with those Gavin had left behind. He wondered at the game Luthias was playing, but as long as no harm came to Curran while they were there, Tanis wasn't going to protest. It would be a lot easier to see to his lover's needs in a quiet, private room than in the courtyard with the other commoners who managed to get inside the gates before they were closed and readied for a long siege.

Luthias was smart in that respect at least. The men among the commoners would fight just as fiercely to protect the walls as the guards who were trained and paid for that very purpose. Free labor...all he had to do was feed them. Tanis knew in time that would become hard, if the siege went on too long. He'd worry about that later. Right now, his only concern was for Curran.

Curran's body gave off more heat than the fire in the stone fireplace. In his feverish delusions, he alternately pushed and tugged on the blankets until they twisted around him like a coiled snake. For what seemed like the thousandth time since he picked the young man's body up from the riverbank, Tanis worked to free him.

"So, you've given up chasing rabbits for the role of nursemaid, I see. Shall I find you in the scullery, hiding behind the skirts of the serving wenches next?"

Tanis kept his back to Luthias, a sign of contempt that the Duke was not perceived as a threat. "I thought my actions were beneath your notice."

"For you, I would not trouble to glance up if you chanced to cross under my nose. It is Curran who draws me."

"What does it matter to you whether he has crossed over to Avalon or not?"

"How dare you mention the burial place of heathens in my presence," Luthias thundered. "Christ strengthens my arm in our darkest hour. None shall speak of another God in my presence, or they shall pay for the sacrilege with their lives."

Though the Duke professed anger, Tanis knew Luthias so well that he also caught the tang of fear in the air. As if his precious Christ would abandon him for consorting with children of another God. And perhaps he would, Tanis reflected, but if so, then his Christ was a very unforgiving sort.

Curran moaned then, preventing Tanis from voicing his opinion to the Duke. Curran had slipped into another fever-dream. His hand groped over the sheets, searching and unsatisfied until he found the hunt master's hand. The sigh of relief bolstered Tanis' conviction not to do or say anything that would get him swept away from the young man's side.

"So how is he then?" Luthias asked impatiently. "Does he improve?"

"Aye, slowly though." Tanis rubbed his thumb over the pale skin on the back of Curran's hand.

"Has he spoken?"

Ah, so that was the real reason behind Luthias' concern. Tanis wondered what tales the young warrior would have to tell when he woke. "Not as yet, your Grace."

"Inform me when he does."

"He will be weaker than a nursing pup. He will be of no use to you."

"My plans for Sir Curran are not your concern. Just see that I am kept informed about his progress."

"I would say he has given enough of himself for you already. Why not let him be?"

"All men must make sacrifices in times of war. When he returns to good health, I expect him to join me."

When Tanis would have jerked out of Curran's grasp to face the Duke, the young warrior hung on with a strength that belied his weakened condition. Tanis didn't see any signs of stirring, but he couldn't bring himself to forcefully part from Curran. He clung to his lover's hand and said, "I will be sure an' tell him."

Angrily, the Duke snapped, "Be equally sure you understand the consequences if he does not. His pledge only ends with death...his or mine."

The Duke made his exit, his regal gait marred by the intermediate thumping of his wooden walking stick he'd taken to carrying with him at all times.

Tanis closed his eyes and concentrated on regulating his breathing. His heart burned to bring divine justice down on the pompous fool's head, preferably with the same end of that pointy stick that had nearly castrated him. His body longed to slide under the sheets and scoop the warrior into his arms, as if that would shield him from further harm. Since neither would currently be of help to Curran, Tanis settled for closing the heavy door and bracing it with a stout length of wood.

He made use of the chamber pot before returning to Curran's pallet in front of the meager fire. The lack of restless noises issuing from the warrior alarmed him. His heart raced for a different reason when he realized Curran was awake.

"Bloody hell, you gave me a scare," Tanis claimed, unable to keep the tears at bay. It was *so* good to see his lover's blue eyes again.

The young warrior struggled to reach out to touch his face. Tanis made it easier by leaning over and pressing the too-warm palm against his grizzled cheek.

"Am I dreaming?" Curran asked.

"'Tis the stuff of nightmares you be looking at, I am sure. But you are not dreaming. You have come back to me at last."

"You are as thin as a shade," Curran replied, his arm dropping to the bed of straw.

Tanis grunted. "Meat is scarce when the hunter becomes the hunted."

"What do you mean?"

But the warrior's blue eyes were sinking under heavy lids. Soon, Curran was back in the land of dreams and Tanis could put off the explanation for another time.

 G8I08I0

Curran faded in and out over the next few days. When he was finally able to sit up, he seemed much more interested in bowls of watery gruel and just being cuddled against Tanis' big body than in any conversation about recent events. Neither one spoke of the incident that caused him such bodily harm, nor of the dire situation they found themselves in. Tanis could almost fool himself into believing that they were living in a cloister, far above the concerns of mortal men. Almost.

The daily clashes along the tower and the deep shadows that crossed Curran's face when he thought Tanis couldn't see him were all that prevented the dream from becoming real. The longer the siege went on, the harder it was to shut out its effects. The women in the courtyard howled in anguish every time a loved one fell to sword or disease. The servants, half-starved and hopeless, brought them meals that got more meager every day. Half his daily rations went into Curran's bowl and the remainder was barely enough to keep him going. Once Curran caught on, he put a stop to it, but it made Tanis more determined than ever to shield him from any other stressful factors.

Curran wasn't one to sit quietly by while others suffered. As soon as he was able, he insisted on touring the grounds. Step by step, he forced himself to go beyond what Tanis considered healthy. Tanis had no idea why Curran was so driven to recover. The fact that Luthias saw his progress and encouraged him didn't help.

The nights were almost worse. Curran would fall asleep only to rage against demons he claimed he couldn't remember upon waking. He'd turn into Tanis' comforting arms and beg for his touch. At those times his passion was almost fierce. Their bodies joined with a desperate tension that didn't entirely snap with release. Curran would again fall into slumber, but his lithe body would remain rigid and ready for battle.

Tanis wished he had the skills of a powerful witch so he could look inside the mind of his lover to see what troubled him so greatly. Since he lacked that skill, he turned to teaching as a means of distraction. He recruited commoners who showed an aptitude for healing to his classes, and turned the care of the wounded mainly over to them.

Luthias paid his activities little attention. His infrequent visits to the areas outside his well-protected audience chamber were mainly to question Curran about the castle's defense. Tension was thick between the two men whenever they met, but with so many witnesses in the area they kept whatever trouble existed between them deeply buried.

Tanis could do nothing but watch and wait and hope that the siege would end soon.

CB∞ℵ

It was perhaps a month into the siege when Tanis began to notice another disturbing change in Curran. The man became more reclusive. He started spending time by himself. He offered excuses for his prolonged absences, many of which were feeble at best. From time to time Tanis feared Curran had found another lover, as he often returned from his trips disheveled. However, he continued to share Tanis' bed and often sought him out for physical comfort. It was only his thoughts that he refused to share.

It seemed best not to challenge him or try to track him when he wandered off, as Tanis didn't want to give him reason to shut him out of his life entirely. Luthias, however, was not so accepting of Curran's surreptitious activities. He was frustrated by his inability to put his hands on the young knight at his every whim. This made for some tense confrontations, but with so many enemies outside the gates, Luthias had plenty of fodder upon which to vent his rage. If the Duke was reduced to toothless growling, Tanis wouldn't interfere.

Still, he worried about Curran. His cares must have shown more than he thought, for one night as the young man crawled into their bed after another long absence, he pressed his hand over Tanis' heart and softly said, "Have faith in me."

"Aye, I do." It wasn't a lie. Tanis preferred to believe that whatever Curran was about was for the best of motives. Twice before he should have trusted in love and the brave men who held his heart. Twice he'd paid a soul-crushing price for his pride and lack of faith. Until he had stark evidence to the contrary, Tanis vowed he would not betray his beloved again.

"It will only be a little while longer, I should think."

"Long or short, as long as you are with me, I will survive."

Tanis guided his lover into his arms. Their legs entwined, and Curran stroked a calloused hand over Tanis' bare chest. "You are the best of men, my love."

"I am nothing without you," he whispered into the thick mane of hair against his cheek.

They couldn't hold out much longer. The castle's exterior was starting to show signs of wear, the people who manned the walls were thinning far too rapidly. Food, even when Athena flew far off to hunt, was becoming frighteningly scarce. Something had to give soon...

Chapter Fourteen
~ *Lies and Truth* ~

Curran rubbed his hands together over the small fire he'd built in the hearth. He hated leaving Tanis out of his plans, but holding these secretive meetings in the hunt master's cabin somehow assuaged some of his guilt. Memories of their lovemaking here, combined with the little personal touches that bespoke of the man who'd dwelled in it for so many years, kept him calm during these most difficult times.

An owl's watchful coo alerted him that company was coming. The man he was to meet was almost as good at skulking about as he was, and Curran was glad that Tanis had taught him to read nature's signs.

Tanis. He couldn't have gotten this far without the man's love, his strength. He knew his recent behavior troubled his lover, but he hoped that once he discovered the reasons for all the secrets he'd be able to forgive him for the deception.

And that Luthias' reign of terror would be over.

Funny, thinking back on it now, that Luthias was really the one responsible for his own downfall. He'd ordered that Gavin's body be left on the field to be scavenged by carrion eaters. Curran could find no one who had seen the brave knight's corpse firsthand. He'd been felled amidst a tight crush of northern raiders who seemed to be brutally attacking him, of that the witnesses all agreed. But no one actually saw him after he went down in a tangle of limbs.

If only there had been a body...but Curran couldn't let the question rest. What had really happened to Gavin?

It was the lack of proof that had Curran considering other fates for the knight he'd been chosen to replace. If he hadn't died, what else might Gavin be doing? Could he have switched sides? Could he possibly be The Lowlander the other prisoners had spoken about? If so, why did he order Tanis' capture?

Finding answers to those questions hadn't been easy. Or safe. Sneaking out of the castle to meet with the enemy could have gotten him killed in any number of gruesome ways, particularly if Luthias had ever learned of his treachery. But he knew his only key to knocking the Duke off his throne lay in forging a truce with the Celts.

It had taken a lot of work to gain their trust. He was repeatedly frustrated by having to work through middlemen instead of dealing directly with their leader. And then, finally, he'd been granted an audience with The Lowlander.

It was hard to say who was more surprised. Though he had long suspected based on the clues he gathered that Gavin was alive and leading the men who now surrounded the Duke's castle, it was a shock to actually see him alive. Gavin later admitted that he never suspected another of the Duke's men would be willing to risk their lives betraying him. Those Luthias didn't rule by his public reputation for kindness were often kept hobbled by fear of his private reputation for utter ruthlessness.

One meeting led to another, and another, until between them they'd formed a workable plan to free the borderlands from Luthias' perverse pastime. Tonight would be the last occasion. If their plans were successful, it would be the start of a new way of life for many. If they lost...

The cabin's sturdy door suddenly opened, and four fur-covered forms staggered in, shaking Curran out of his dark study. The tallest of the three pulled back his hood to reveal a halo of golden hair and glittering green-blue eyes. It was a face he found startlingly like his own, the face of the man who Tanis loved before him.

Curran stood, keeping his sword hand unobtrusively near the hilt of his weapon. Though they'd met several times before, neither one took for granted that their next conversation would end cordially. That was how smart men stayed alive in these troubled times.

"Gavin," Curran said formally, as the others stomped their feet and shrugged their shoulders to rid themselves of accumulated snow. "I thought the snow might delay you."

"Mother Nature will not stand in my way now, not when we are so close to our goal." He walked to the fire to warm his hands and feet. "Are you ready?"

"I know the recipe for the drug Tanis uses to ease the pain of the wounded and put them in a healing trance. I can only guess as to how much it will take to subdue all the people inside the walls, but I have the supplies for brewing more than a thousand doses."

"How many of you are left?"

Curran hesitated. Giving out that kind of information could be detrimental to his health and further endanger those who remained. If Gavin thought he could overpower the force, there would be no need to go through this potentially ruinous ruse. On the other hand, the people inside the walls were the very people they were working to save. Just because they didn't realize who their true enemy was didn't mean they should pay for that ignorance with their lives.

"Less than half the original number," Curran finally admitted. "The winter has been as dangerous an enemy as you. Food is scarce, and the living conditions are becoming dire."

"And yet Luthias still lives in comfort, like a happy, contented cat in his bower while the world crumbles around him."

Curran remained silent. There wasn't much point in confirming what they both knew to be true.

Gavin turned from the fire to face him. Light flickered against his profile, bringing more beauty out of his handsome features. He was lean and battle-hardened, smart yet compassionate. Everything an honorable knight should be. "I will move heaven and earth to put an end to his evil ways. Are you equally committed?"

"I am."

"And who do you fancy for the throne once the old Duke has been ousted?"

"I presumed you yourself would take control of the duchy. Between your family lineage and your friends at court, you will no doubt gain the king's approval."

The other three men—clan leaders who were there to carry word of what was discussed back to their families—grunted in approval. Any man who had put his life in their hands, given them hope that the Duke's war games could end in their favor, and offered to show them how could certainly be trusted to leave their remaining possessions alone. That's all the Highlanders wanted, really. Was to be left alone.

No more border raids, no more sieges. No more needless bloodshed. Curran dreamed of the day when that would happen, and he and Tanis would be free to return to this cabin in the woods and live as lovers.

Assuming Tanis didn't choose Gavin over him, and on that point Curran was far from certain.

"I am not the healer this land needs," Gavin replied. "I am a warrior, prone to answer any slight with my blade rather than my brain. These people will benefit most from a man capable of drawing out the best from them, someone who can unify them in times of trial and give them hope. Someone they already respect and look to for advice. Can you think of no one who fits that description better than I?"

"Tanis." Damn. Gavin wanted to put the hunt master on the duchy's throne.

Curran couldn't deny that Tanis would make a great duke. No other person on the castle grounds, not even Luthias himself, garnered more praise and devotion than Tanis these days. People naturally warmed to him when he allowed it. His towering strength and quiet nature made it easy for people to share their troubles with him. He had only to ask for a thing, and it was done. The people would support him in ways few others could match. Curran had to admit, now that he thought about it, Tanis was the best choice they had. The best choice for Otterburn.

But what of him and their future?

Perhaps that's why Gavin had been so strangely insistent on confirming that he was committed to the cause. Would he still be willing to help if it meant losing Tanis? Curran searched his heart and found only one answer. Yes. He loved Tanis deeply, but when compared to the lives of hundreds, his desires didn't matter.

"It is his rightful place," Gavin added.

Curran's eyes drifted toward the bed where they'd once made love. Until this moment, he'd always pictured that bed as their *rightful place*. Quelling the pain welling up from his soul, he asked, "How so? Luthias was next in line for the duchy, was he not?"

"Luthias is older, that much is true. Luthias, however, is not the son of Isolade, Duke Osric's first wife. Isolade died shortly after giving birth to Tanis, and Osric married again. This new bride came to him with a son from a previous marriage. Her husband had been killed by the *heathens* and by marrying her Osric gained the support of a staunch ally in his battles against the northern raiders. Luthias was raised as his own flesh and blood, but Tanis is the only one who carries Osric's blood."

"Then why did the Duke not name Tanis as his heir?"

"Osric saw in Luthias the son that Tanis would never be. Luthias shared his hatred of the Highlanders, whereas Tanis wanted to befriend them. Even as children, Luthias aped Osric's high-handed ways while Tanis soothed those who were hurt by his father's cruel words. Luthias may not have been the son of his loins, but he was the son of that bastard's evil heart." Love and admiration for the hunt master shone from Gavin's eyes.

"What if that holds true today? What if Tanis refuses to take the crown?"

"He will not like it, but he will bow to necessity. He would no more stand aside and let this land suffer than he would refuse to treat a wounded animal."

"True that," Curran grudgingly admitted.

"And when Tanis accepts the mantle of Duke, I will take my place at his side."

Curran felt Gavin's commanding stare and raised his chin so their eyes met. Since his clan leaders were behind him, they couldn't see the double meaning those words had. Gavin planned on resuming their intimate relationship as well as their political one.

Curran couldn't blame him for that, not one bit. In Gavin's place, he would feel the same. Without a doubt, Tanis would be overjoyed to see that his old lover had not cast off his mortal coil after all. Would the memories of old times be enough to supplant Curran in his bed?

"Once I am with him again, I will see to it that he has no need for you." Gavin spoke so low that Curran could scarcely see his lips moving. "Do not deceive yourself on this point, Sir Curran. Tanis' heart has always belonged to me, and mine to him."

"He is not the man you once knew," Curran replied just as quietly. "What if he no longer desires you above all others?"

"Then I will fight for him in the bedroom with the same skill and determination I use on the battlefield. If you have any love for him at all, you will stand aside peacefully and not make him choose. We both know that I am better suited to be his helpmate once he takes control of the duchy and I will allow no one to come between us."

Curran held that fierce gaze for a long second before he finally looked away. Gavin was right. Even if Tanis did, by some miracle, prefer a young, starry-eyed swordsman to a brave, experienced knight, Curran would be of little help to him in the running of the keep, or any of the other ruling tasks he'd be obligated to master. His only experience at being a cultured individual was based on what he'd picked up from Evander and the items Gavin had left behind. He had no political connections or courtly manner, nothing to aid Tanis in his new role.

If they could stay as guardsman and hunt master, Curran would never leave his side. If love had any sway at all, they'd ride through this political tempest together. But Curran feared that duty would again win out over love, and that bowing to necessity would be Tanis' best option for success.

The duchy would gain a Duke they could be proud of, and Curran would gain naught but a broken heart.

Gavin stepped back and raised his voice. "I give you one last chance to break your word without consequence. If you have not the stomach for what will happen next, say the word and I will find another way into the castle."

With a rising tide of sorrow filling his soul, Curran replied, "I am with you."

Chapter Fifteen
~ *Cementing Alliances* ~

Curran made no move to see Gavin again. There was no need. The plans were set. All they waited for was the signal that Gavin had his troops in place. Instead of skulking about, Curran spent every free moment with Tanis, dogging his footsteps and offering a helping hand when he could, and thinking upon him with all the love in his heart when he couldn't.

Tanis seemed to appreciate this new behavior, although was equally puzzled by it. Luthias, on the other hand, found it annoying and so he went out of his way to come up with tasks to keep them separated as much as possible. Curran had a hard time hiding his negative feelings for the Duke. Contrary to what he'd told the others, he remembered every single betrayal Luthias had committed. It was all he could do to refrain from running the man through with his sharp blade whenever he had to be in his presence.

Luthias had to remain alive though, Gavin made that very clear. Should the Duke die before Tanis was given his crown, there would be a heated battle between neighboring territories, Luthias' own offspring and the northern raiders. A war that would no doubt leave the countryside in far worse condition than Luthias' evil reign already had. All parties agreed to Tanis as the leader, and thus Tanis it had to be.

But waiting was both a blessing and a curse. Each day he had with Tanis was a treasure. Each day they were forced to endure Luthias' sick and twisted machinations was pure hell. True, the evil man was almost toothless during the siege, having lost more than half of his subjects to war and disease, and having to hide his true nature so he didn't offend the rest. However, he made his barbs felt, and Curran didn't think the world could be rid of him soon enough.

Then, the night the signal came in the form of a truce, Curran found it was happening all too soon. He had one more night with his heart's true love. One more night with their bodies joined as tightly as their souls, and Curran planned to make the most of it.

"Did you hear?" Tanis said as he entered their private chamber. "The clansmen have agreed to negotiate. They will bring food to show their good intent, and all Luthias has to do is refrain from firing on them as they approach."

He kissed Tanis soundly, happy to see the heavily lined face he loved so well wearing something other than a grimace. "I heard."

"Tonight we shall eat, drink and be merry, for tomorrow we shall be free!"

He laughed and turned Curran around in a circle. Curran swallowed the lump of emotion in his throat. Now was not the time to bawl like a woman over spilled milk. He had to accept that he'd lost Tanis to his future, and he wouldn't ruin their last minutes together by fighting it.

"I am to oversee the transfer of foodstuffs through the gate," Curran told him. "I will meet you back here when I am through so that we may celebrate this good fortune in private. Does that suit you?"

"Aye, it does."

Tanis embraced him and Curran could feel the hard length of his shaft pressing against his thigh. His mouth watered at the thought of swallowing that ruddied head until it hit the back of his throat. He wanted to wrap his legs around Tanis' hips and be taken hard and fast like their first time, to let his love pour through their connection and feed on his thick, white come.

He grabbed Tanis by the shirt and held on tight. "Promise me you won't allow a drop of wine or a bite of meat to pass your lips until I am with you."

"I swear it," Tanis replied fiercely. "Be quick about your business though, my Curran, for I am in the mood to devour you."

After another long kiss that caused his cock to harden and his heart to pound, Curran raced out of the room. He put Evander in charge of the servants and made short work of transferring the casks of ale and other goods inside the castle walls. The whole time Curran could feel Luthias' eyes on his back. The scruff of his neck itched, but Luthias kept to his promise and refrained from firing upon his chosen enemy.

That was the only part Curran couldn't control. If Luthias gave the order to fire despite flying a flag of truce, they'd all be dead. The only hope Curran had was that Luthias would bask in his apparent victory, leaving revenge for a future date. All he needed was a short delay...

For once the evil Duke kept his word, and Curran was too relieved to question it. His mind was focused on his last task, and then he would be free to enjoy Tanis' lovemaking until near dawn.

"Evander, send a few barrels to the courtyard and another brace to the guardsmen's barracks," Curran instructed his friend. "Some of the salted beef as well."

"Yes, sir."

"There will be a flood of bodies after the bounty. Do your best to keep them well fed. They must not raid the cellars, or we will have more bloodshed."

"Understood, sir."

"And once you have completed your duties, I want you to take a cask to share with the kitchen staff. Drink tonight as if you were a king." It was the best warning Curran could give the loyal servant.

"Evil festers more than ever in the stones of this cursed place, but I think that for once we have beaten the devil at his own game. For that, I would drink a toast to the bowels of Hell." He offered Curran a rare, quick smile before backing out of the storage room to attend to his chores.

Curran listened at the stairs, but there was only one set of footsteps to be heard and those quickly faded away. He went in the opposite direction, to the cell where he once nearly lost his life. It seemed a fitting place to store the sleeping draught that would bring about another life-altering change. The stench of rotting corpses—for the chamber was now used as a place to store the decaying bodies of those who'd died inside the keep—caused him to gag. But it was another reason he thought the hiding place was apt. The smell alone would keep out the curious.

It looked like a bottle of cooking oil, and so it wouldn't cause suspicion if someone met him along the way back to the storage room. Again Curran was lucky. He encountered no one, and so he was able to get to work straightaway.

It seemed as though there were thousands of casks rather than the twenty-five they'd agreed upon. Curran carefully opened each one, added a measure of the medication and then re-corked it. He was nearly finished when the rustle of fabric alerted him to the fact that he had company.

"What are you about?" Luthias demanded.

He clung to the walls like a frightened child. Curran suspected it was because he was so weak and frail from illness rather than fear. Still, it made him look small instead of the larger-than-life man Curran was used to seeing.

"Testing for poison."

"Ah, so you suspect the northern dogs of treachery too?"

No, you miserable bastard. It is you I mistrust. "Better to be cautious than dead."

Luthias laughed. "Cautious? You? Has this long siege stripped you of your courage, boy?"

"It has taught me there are more important things in life than winning." Curran knew he should hold his tongue, but standing on the cusp of victory made him fear no evil. If there was yet a God in Heaven, this would be Luthias' last day as Duke. The thought made him weak-kneed and loose-lipped.

"Rubbish," the Duke declared with a broad sweep of his hand. It left him unbalanced and he had to scramble to clasp at the wall again. "Nothing on this earth rivals the glory to be found in winning."

"What about losing?" Curran asked quietly. "What joy is there to be found in that?"

"None, my dear Curran. That is why I will do whatever it takes to succeed."

His eyes glittered, and Curran could almost see the shadows moving behind them. The dark intentions that had brought so much evil to the land. When he spoke it was really to them rather than the human husk they inhabited. "Life is precious. There are ways to win without death."

"Yes, but they are not nearly so entertaining." Luthias crossed the floor in a pitiful gait that mocked his once powerful stride. Curran forgot to be wary of this frail-seeming creature and therefore was caught unawares when the Duke grabbed him by the balls. "You have big ones. I can teach you how to use them. How to be a king among men."

"I have no desire to rule."

Luthias' grip became tighter even as his face turned thoughtful. "I thought that being caged with the savages would have disabused you of your noble notions yet you continue to defend them. Perhaps you have not been properly motivated to walk in my footsteps after all."

Curran reached for the Duke's genitals and applied the same amount of pressure. "Perhaps you'd do well to leave me in peace."

The Duke's eyes turned angry and cold. Curran knew his life hung in the balance. Then the man released him with a short, barking laugh. "As I said, you have big ones, Curran. I will make a worthy man out of you yet." He didn't turn away, but rather stepped backward until he reached the doorway. "Keep in mind that I still own you, Curran. Once the human sheep are herded from my castle gate, I expect you to return to your duties at my side."

"I understand, your Grace." *And I will not obey.* Should the worst come to pass and Gavin's coup failed, Curran would die by his own sword than be a part of Luthias' atrocities.

"I pray that you do. I would hate to lose a good hunt master in order to make my meaning clear to you."

Luthias disappeared up the stairs. It took all of Curran's self-control not to rush the man and squeeze the life from his body for suggesting that he'd have Tanis killed. Right warred with wrong as he listened to the sound of leather scraping against stone. It wouldn't take much effort to end it all here, now.

But that would make him no better than the man he loathed like the very devil.

Several long moments of deep breathing restored a measure of his control. He then hurried through the rest of the kegs until the bottle of sleeping draught was emptied. The cask he'd set aside to share with Tanis went untreated. He stuffed a bit of dried beef into his pocket, then bent over to pick it up. As he did, he spotted a scrawny old rat hiding behind it. At once it reminded him of Luthias.

It took several attempts before he was able to grab it and stuff it in his pocket. Athena was entitled to a celebratory meal too.

Chapter Sixteen
~ *One Last Kiss* ~

Curran returned to the room he shared with Tanis, carrying the untainted cask under one arm and a handful of salted beef in the other, praying the hunt master had done as he'd asked. His trust was well placed. Tanis was not only waiting for him, but he'd gone so far as to set the stage for seduction in as much as their meager supplies would allow. Fresh straw for their bed, and a change of clothes for himself. He'd washed his hair and face, and the refuse they'd been piling in the corners of the room during the long, dreary months had been removed. Even the window—which had been closed to prevent stray arrows from finding a target—was open to the day's cool air. It made the space a bit chilly, but seeing the sunlight pouring in did wonderful things to Tanis' appearance.

By comparison, Curran felt like he was wearing a dung heap. Though Luthias' touch had left no visible stains, he refused to approach his lover until he'd bathed. This would be their last time together, if Gavin had his way. He didn't want anything to spoil that.

Tanis met him halfway across the room, and eased the small keg from his arms. "So it went well then?"

Curran nodded as he crossed over to the hearth and set the hunks of beef on the mantle. The fire burned low since kindling would remain in short supply until they had time to scavenge in the woods for it. It would take months to set the castle to rights after most of its contents had been sacrificed for survival. What would their lives be like come spring?

Bleaker than the past winter, if I do not have Tanis to love.

"Why do you look so sad, my love? Are you not happy that we will soon be free of this place?"

Not we. Just me. "I ran across Luthias on my raid of the larder."

Tanis reached him in two long strides and grabbed his shoulders. "Did he hurt you?"

"No, he was merely his unpleasant self."

Tanis' hands slid along the muscles of his shoulders toward his neck. They rose to cup his jaw from both sides. The heat of the hunt master's hands poured much-needed warmth back into Curran's soul. It was always like this when they touched, and Curran knew it was one of many things he'd miss about Tanis when they parted ways.

"I wish you would not wander the halls alone. You make an easy target without someone to watch your back," Tanis said quietly.

"I promise I will not leave this room again without you, for as long as you wish it." It was an easy promise to make. They didn't have much time together left.

Tanis' eyes widened in surprise, but he quickly replied, "I will hold you to that."

Their lips met to seal the promise. Curran still had plans to wash before they went too far, but all practical thoughts faded as Tanis enveloped him in a warm embrace. Their bodies fit together so well. Even through several layers of heavy clothing, Curran could feel Tanis' solid muscle pressing against him.

"Curran," Tanis murmured against his lips, "please tell me that it is not a rat you have in your pocket."

Curran burst out laughing. He couldn't help it. He fished the poor excuse for a rat out of his pants and held it up by the tail. "Oh, but it is, you see."

"And why, pray tell, did you choose to keep it there?"

"I found it in the storeroom. I did not wish Athena to be left out of the celebration, but I had no other way to carry it since my hands were full."

"You thought of her?" Tanis asked with a note of wonder in his voice.

"Of course. She is a part of you."

"A bird, a pet, most would not bother to notice," Tanis mumbled. "You are a prince among men, Curran Aurick."

That was too close to Luthias' statement for Curran's comfort. He dangled the rat in front of Tanis' nose as if to entice him into taking a bite. "Perhaps you would like to feed your friend while I bathe. Then you and I will feast."

"Be quick about it," Tanis growled as he swiped the pest up into his own fist.

Someone had brought them a pail of water—melted snow from outside the castle walls, Curran suspected—and Tanis had warmed it by the fire. Curran made quick use of it, scrubbing away what seemed like years of accumulated dirt from his skin. Off to the side, he heard Tanis call for Athena with the old familiar cry. The hawk replied in kind from somewhere in the distance, and soon he heard the flutter of wings at the window.

"Good fortune to you, my friend," Tanis crooned to her. "Eat and be well."

Curran glanced over and saw the rat fly out of the window. No doubt Athena, with her keen sight, would snatch it from the air. Tanis drew the wooden shutters closed, then pulled the heavy drapes over them. "Do you mind?"

"Mind?"

"Shutting out the light again. We have been in the dark for so long, but I find I wish to keep you all to myself."

"No, I do not mind."

Tanis returned to his side in measured steps. Their eyes remained locked. When they were toe-to-toe, Tanis tugged on the wet, rough rag in his hand. "Allow me."

"I am nearly done," Curran protested. "Besides, I would think you would be glad to turn over such a menial task as this back to me."

"I will never tire of having my hands on you."

Curran's heart wept to hear such beautiful words. Everything he ever dreamed about hearing from the Duke's lips back when he was young and naive could be found in the man who stood before him now. One didn't have to wear a crown to be noble or courageous. He just had to be strong and brave. And there was no one Curran knew who was stronger or braver than Tanis in body, mind and soul.

"Make love to me," Curran urged him. "I need to feel your body joined with mine."

Tanis' lips curved up in a rare smile. "It would be my greatest pleasure."

No bruising kiss or frantic grasping followed. Tanis took his time peeling away the remainder of Curran's clothes. Then he went on to bathe him. Front to back, Tanis kept up a trickle of warm water and light scrubbing that left Curran feeling raw and exposed. The rough texture of the fabric scraped lightly over his skin, arousing his senses. His lover's unblinking attention kept him rooted to the spot. His body was no longer as pretty as when they'd first met. He had plenty of battle scars, but Tanis paid them no more attention than he did any other spots. It was as if Tanis was trying to impress upon him the fact that he accepted Curran as a whole being, not just limiting his love to a few choice bits.

"What do you see in me?" The question slipped out before Curran even realized he was going to ask it.

"A man with the heart of a lion, the soul of a poet and the body of an angel."

His words brought an old memory to surface, from the first time they were together. "Am I no longer the devil then, sent to tempt you beyond your limits?"

"Aye, that too." Tanis made a noise that sounded like an attempt to clear his throat. "And...uhm...in me? Is there something worthy you find in this aging body?"

The cloth stopped brushing against his back, and Curran turned to face Tanis. "The man I love beyond all reason. The person who occupies the center of my world and the keeper of my heart."

Tanis' dark eyes sparked with unshed tears. "Soul of a damned poet, just as I said."

"It is nothing to string a few words together in a pleasing way. It is the actions of a man when no one is looking that speaks volumes about who he is. I have seen you when you thought no one was watching, Tanis. I know your heart is good and true. You are a fair man, an honest man. And the only man I love."

Tanis slid his arms around his waist. One hand came up to fist in his long blond hair, the other went to the base of his spine where a slight pressure brought their bodies together. "Love you, my brave lion."

Curran's reply was lost in their kiss. The first invading thrust of Tanis' tongue sent a stab of pure lust to

Curran's groin. It pulsed and throbbed as blood rushed to fill it.

Tanis paused for breath. "That better be no damn rat."

"No, love. Not this time. Just my need for you."

He grunted in teasing satisfaction, then returned to his deeply passionate kisses. Curran lost all sense of time and place in his arms. The feel of work-roughened skin over his buttocks and back sent shivers down his spine. He longed to be thrown upon the hay-strewn floor and taken roughly, but at the same time he found this slow approach to be infinitely seductive.

"Skin. Let me touch you," Curran begged of him.

Tanis' heavy leather jerkin was cast aside in a matter of heartbeats. Curran caressed the mat of soft hair on his chest while Tanis stripped off his fur-lined pants. Amber light from the fire washed over his skin as it was revealed, setting it aglow. Curran's mouth watered to get his hands on it. Even before he straightened up from casting his pants aside, Curran was on him. Hands glided over every curve of muscle, every lean line of his frame. He pressed open-mouthed kisses against Tanis' shoulders. And finally, when he could, he closed his mouth around one dusky male nipple and lashed at the sensitive tip with his tongue.

"Ah, Curran, what you do to me is pure heaven."

Though long fingers tangled in his hair, they didn't tug or otherwise urge him to change his course. He followed the dart of dark hair down his chest. His hands moved with him, caressing the firm flesh of his lower back. He stopped there to massage the tense muscles just under the surface as his tongue delved into Tanis' bellybutton. It was a surprise to them both when Curran discovered how the odd notch could be used as a sensual weapon. Now he had enough practice to draw a strangled groan of pleasure from his lover's lips, just by tongue-fucking the shallow hole.

The head of Tanis' shaft beat against Curran's chest, begging for attention. He left a trail of kisses in his wake as he lowered his head to that impressive organ. So finely crafted it was that God himself must have had a hand in its creation, Curran thought. Long and thick, powerfully built as the rest of the man. Curran fit his lips over it as he imagined it filling his arse.

The blood-engorged flesh felt hot against his tongue. The dorsal vein pulsed against his lips as they slid up and down the meaty shaft. Tanis began to rock his hips, slowly but insistently. Curran guided his hips, not yet wanting to take him in deeply.

"Suck me, Curran. Deep and hard like I know you can."

The fat head slipped out from between his lips. He turned his head from side to side, letting the sensitive skin graze over his stubbled cheeks. "No."

"Why not?" Tanis demanded.

"It will go easier with some ale."

He crawled to the cask in a panther's gait. He worked the cork free, then turned to find a drinking vessel. Tanis

173

had one ready for him, and Curran filled it to the brim. On his knees before Tanis, he tipped the cup and spilled a mouthful of the intoxicating drink over his lover's thick length.

Aside from a soft grunt of surprise, Tanis made no attempt to dissuade him from continuing. Curran licked the droplets from his balls.

"By the Gods, man..." Tanis said hoarsely.

Curran drizzled another sip of the amber liquid onto Tanis' cock then sucked the rivulets from his scrotum. The tang was so much stronger with Tanis' unique flavor added to it. It made his head spin. His thumbs dug into the scars surrounding his sex as he greedily chased down more of the intoxicating mix. The forest of fine curls hid the worst of them, but the pain they must have caused him brought another wave of tenderness to his heart.

"Enough of your teasing." Tanis' foot suddenly connected with his shoulder, and Curran went over, tumbling onto a pile of soft straw. Ale splashed against his chest as the cup flew out of his hand. He barely had time to register this shift in circumstances before Tanis fell upon him.

"My turn to sample Dionysus' brew," Tanis declared. Curran's chest was treated to a long swipe of Tanis' tongue. "Hmmm. I see why you are so fond of the stuff."

He went back to licking and nibbling. Curran brought Tanis' fingers to his mouth and sucked on each digit to ensure that no sticky residue remained. His tongue swirled over the sensitive tips. He licked the webbing between them. Then he started sliding the first digit in and out of his mouth as if foretelling what was to come.

Tanis moved up his body until chest was pressed to chest. Tanis' solid thighs bracketed his. Their cocks nestled together between their bodies. It was amazing how alive he felt in the hunt master's arms, and how cold and lonely he was when he and Tanis were apart.

"Fill me up, lover. So full that I will never be without you," Curran mumbled around his fingers.

"Nothing will part us, ever," Tanis swore. He slammed his mouth down over Curran's and it seemed as though he was trying to pour every ounce of his love into him. Hungry and hot, their mouths mated. Curran fisted his hands in Tanis' hair and clung to him desperately. He lifted his hips, insisting on more. More love. More of Tanis. Just plain *more*.

Rolling onto his back, Tanis took Curran with him. He swept Curran's hair back, over his shoulder, with a gentle brush of his hand. "I watched you ride off on Luthias' crusade," he admitted softly. "It was torture to let you leave without knowing whether or not you'd return." He thrust up, grinding his cock against Curran's belly. "Torture too watching your sweet arse rock in the saddle, wishing I was the animal under you."

"I never knew—" He tried to swallow the lump in his throat and tried again. "You never said—" He still couldn't get the words out.

"So cool and remote. You wore the face of a warrior. I could not touch you then, but I can now." Tanis grabbed his hips and pulled him down against his crotch. "Ride me, Curran. Ride me home."

Curran reached between them to find his lover's cock. Slick with ale, sweat and pre-come, they needed nothing else to ease the way. Curran rose above it, then impaled himself upon it, inch by delicious inch. There wasn't much give to the mighty organ as it invaded his body. Though he'd become accustomed to Tanis' girth, his body still had to stretch to admit him. He hissed in pleasure/pain as the head of his cock pushed past the tight ring of muscle.

"Yes, lover, take all of me." Tanis ran his hands over Curran's thighs.

Burning passion seared him from the inside out. He shuddered from the wealth of sensations. Tanis under him. The crude words that urged him on. The musky smell of sex in the air. Pre-come pearled up from his slit and slowly oozed down the length of his shaft.

He planted his hands on Tanis' hairy chest to steady himself as he moved up and down that rigid pole of flesh. His muscles easily slid into the rolling gait of a rider on horseback.

Tanis lifted his hips off the straw to give him deeper penetration. "So long I have dreamed of having you like this. You are a dream come true."

"No dream, no vision. This is real. *I* am real, and so is my love for you."

They rarely spoke so openly to each other. It was too easy to be overheard in a castle that was packed with people of all stations. To share a private room was one thing, but to advertise their feelings was not wise. On this occasion, however, Curran saw no need for restraint. By now the drug would have taken effect on most of the revelers. And even if he was heard, he doubted he'd be around long enough for any real trouble to be caused by it. Tanis loved him now but that was sure to change once he found out Gavin was alive.

And if nothing else, Tanis would hate him for keeping that knowledge a secret for so long.

So come tomorrow, Curran would most likely be gone, one way or another. He'd not be silent about his love for the hunt master with only his memories of this time for company on his solitary journey out.

"Come for me here, on my chest," Tanis urged him.

Curran wasn't ready to let go. The base of his spine tingled with warnings of impending release, but he could hold out a little longer...

Tanis' fingers stroked his shaft, a soft touch in contrast to the brute force of his penetrating thrusts. "Come for me."

"Make me," Curran hissed back.

Challenge lit up the hunt master's eyes. "It will be my pleasure."

Curran was quite confused when Tanis pushed him off and stood up. He fished around in the pockets of his discarded leather vest and came up with a pair of jesses. "Against the wall."

There was no room for objection. Tanis advanced, determination written on his face. Curran backed up, unsure about his lover's intent. "What are you going to do with those?"

"Tether you."

Tanis muscled him into the wall and pinned him there with his shoulder. His mouth landed on Curran's and kept it pleasurably occupied while his hands fondled his balls. Curran didn't really pay much attention to what Tanis was doing until he stepped back. He looked down to see his heavy balls lashed together and securely bound. "What are you playing at?"

"Trust me."

"With my life," Curran answered immediately. "But this is..."

"Exactly what you asked for. Now turn around."

Tanis' cock returned to his greedy hole and he began to rock into him with a force that left him stunned. Hard, hot pounding propelled him beyond thought. He braced his arms against the stone and pushed back to meet his every thrust. Tanis pressed his forehead against Curran's spine. One hand gripped his thigh, the other stroked his cock with demanding tugs.

Curran tried to hold back his desire, but Tanis' rough handling turned him on more than he ever thought possible. "You win. I surrender. Release me."

"No."

The steady hammering continued. His arse burned from the rubbing, but in a way that only increased his pleasure. At this angle, Tanis could unerringly hit the special spot inside him that added an extra tingle. Darkness swam at the edge of his vision, and the only piece of life he could connect with was the man who seemed determined to merge their two bodies into one.

His balls were red and so tight with need that they were on the verge of going numb. "Release me," he begged. "Please."

A long, shuddering groan preceded the warm rush of fluid that filled his arse. Tanis swore under his breath as though his release had caught him by surprise. Still, he managed to loosen the leather straps around Curran's balls and that was all it took for him to follow Tanis over the edge.

Curran let out a shout that was sure to bring the guards running if any of them were still awake as come burst from him in long white ropes. Climax wracked his muscles. It hurt to breathe, his heart was pounding so hard. And yet it was the most pleasurable release of his life. His whole body was one big nerve ending, and the way Tanis continued to rub his hands over his skin kept the muscular tremors going much longer than they ever had before.

When he was worn down beyond any ability to hold himself erect, he tumbled over Tanis' chest. He felt the strong arms embrace him. The heat of their bodies made a blanket unnecessary, for now.

"How is it possible that you were so skilled a lover, and yet I never knew the full extent of your talent until tonight?" Curran asked sleepily.

"Why do you assume you know the full extent of it now?" Tanis replied, his voice laced with good humor.

"You mean there is more?"

"Much more, Curran. And I hope you will permit me to spend the rest of my life proving it to you."

As do I.

Curran sank into a light doze, warm and content for the moment, but he knew it wouldn't last. As soon as night reached its darkest hours, Gavin's men would swarm through the halls. And what happened after that was entirely out of his hands.

Chapter Seventeen
~ *Victory* ~

"Come with me," Curran said, waking Tanis from a light doze.

"What is it?"

"There is something I must show you. Please, come."

They delayed long enough to dress in simple clothing with only his hunting knife for their defense. True, the northern raiders were headed home but something about their surrender in the face of victory seemed untrustworthy to Tanis. He'd have felt better if they were both wearing battle gear, but Curran had insisted that he leave all weapons behind.

The night silence was only broken by the sounds of heavy snoring as they crept through the stone halls. Even the servants were nowhere to be seen.

"Where are we going?" Tanis asked him and was immediately shushed.

Curran leaned over to put his mouth against Tanis' ear and spoke so softly it was almost imperceptible from the stillness around them. "Please keep quiet. I would rather not have company just yet. I promise, it will all make sense soon."

Tanis followed in Curran's footsteps, marveling at how well the young man had learned his lessons in skullduggery. He thought at first they might be headed toward the kitchen but they continued beyond the servants' quarters and into a section of the keep Tanis never knew existed. The stairs twisted like a serpent, sometimes so narrow that Tanis had to turn to the side in order to descend.

Then, suddenly, Curran disappeared as if the night had swallowed him whole. A harsh gasp escaped Tanis' lips and he tried to hurry to the spot where he'd last seen his lover. A pair of arms shot out and hauled him backward, dragging him into a tiny room.

"If you ever felt any love in your heart for me at all, you will stay in this room until I come for you." Curran kissed his lips hard, an amazing feat in the almost total darkness. "Promise me?"

"Yes, but—"

Another kiss stopped his words. "Wait for me."

Curran slipped out as quietly as a cat, and then disappeared around the sharp curve of the stairs. He counted the heartbeats pounding through his veins as he waited for sounds of his lover's return. As before, there was no warning when Curran reappeared, just as Tanis' nerves were stretched to the breaking point.

And he was not alone.

"What...what have you done?" Tanis asked as the tiny room filled with the northern savages.

Only five of the short, stocky brutes could fit inside the chamber, and one other who stood head and shoulders above his companions.

"I have brought back the dead," Curran replied.

"Greetings, Tanis," a familiar voice rumbled through the darkness.

His legs trembled. He might even have fallen had there been room, his shock was so great. "Gavin?"

"Aye."

He reached for the man, wanting to touch him, but several strong arms pushed him back and Curran stepped in front of him.

"Harm Tanis and the revolt dies here," Curran growled.

"Revolt?" Things were happening too fast, and Tanis couldn't get a grip on any of it.

Gavin grinned. "Ready for a bit of revenge?"

Tanis didn't have time to answer. A startled shout drew their attention.

"Go, go," Curran urged them. "Remember, do not harm the servants. They are on our side."

The men filed out and charged up the stairs, following Gavin's lead. By the Gods, there seemed to be an endless stream of them, so many more than could have ever fit into that cramped space. Curran pushed Tanis out into the middle of the human flood and they were swept along, into the upper levels of the castle. They were thrust into another room, this one a great deal bigger and lighted by lamps.

There was only one place that still had fuel to burn, and that was Luthias' private quarters. What in the Seven Hells was going on?

"Your reign of terror is at an end, Luthias," Gavin said from his bedside.

As his eyes adjusted to the light, Tanis spotted the Duke lying on his bed. His limbs were painfully stretched by ropes that were anchored to the bedposts. Crimson marks stained his cheeks as though someone had slapped them repeatedly to bring him around.

"Gavin." Luthias' face was deathly pale as he gazed upon his former knight. Whether his reaction was from shock or anger, it was hard to tell. "But, you are dead. I saw your body impaled on a brute's sword with my own eyes."

"You are not the only one skilled at concealing your true nature, Luthias."

Sounds of fighting on the castle grounds drifted up to his ears, but Tanis only heard a buzzing in his head. How had they accomplished this? Like a flood, a river of facts formed connections in his head. Curran's dreams of treachery and death. The Lowlander he spoke of must refer to Gavin but how had Curran managed to locate him? Curran, obviously, had gone through great lengths to help orchestrate the coup. No wonder he'd been so secretive!

His heart burst with love for the strong, young warrior. His faith had not been misplaced.

Unless he'd found something with Gavin...

But no, he had only to look at his former friend to see that Gavin harbored nothing greater than a deep respect for the courageous blond. And Curran paid scant attention to the former knight.

Something inside him...something he thought long dead...began to struggle for freedom. Happiness.

"You will not succeed in this, traitor. My men are loyal. You will be ousted within hours, and I will personally see that your execution is long and painful."

Gavin laughed as he tugged roughly on the signet ring Luthias wore as a sign of his station. "More of your sick delusions, old man? Forgive me for failing to cower, but I have never been one to jump at shadows."

"And who will take my place? You? A ghost?" Luthias' laughter was high-pitched, like that of one whose mind had completely gone.

Curran stepped up to the bed. "No, Luthias. This time, the crown will go to the man most deserving, the one born to wear it."

"Ah, Curran, my beloved. Will you abandon me to these heathens? Has my love and trust meant so little to you?"

"Love? Trust? You defile the words merely by speaking them. You know not their meaning, only the perversions you commit in their name." Tanis was stunned to see the composed mask slip away from his lover's face to reveal the tortured soul underneath. "There is no vow you will not break, not to the land, or the people, or even your God. You are evil, Luthias, and I will spend the rest of my life atoning for the sins I have committed on your orders."

The older man preened, as if Curran's angry denouncement had been a compliment. "Wait until you wear the crown, Curran. Once you have a taste of true power, you will learn that my ways are only for the greater glory of us all."

"There is one much better suited to become the next Duke of Otterburn than I, Luthias. The one you stole the title from so long ago."

Tanis started to get a curious feeling in his stomach, as if his life had been turned inside out and exposed for all to see. He wasn't particularly comfortable with the sensation. He was made even less comfortable when Gavin went down on bended knee and silently held out his hand.

As if it were someone else, Tanis saw his hand reach out for Gavin's.

"With this ring, I declare you Tanis, Fifth Duke of Otterburn," Gavin said solemnly.

"No, he is nothing but a pretender. I will not tolerate this," Luthias howled from his bed.

"Someone silence that man," Gavin ordered. "Spare his life but shut him up."

The world spun in a lazy circle as two men rushed to the bed and stuffed Luthias' mouth with linen from his sheets.

Once his cries were cut off, Gavin repeated his declaration.

"I hereby witness this and swear the rightful man wears the ring," Curran added.

The same statement was echoed around the room as each of Gavin's men repeated the words. The northerners would recognize him as the Fifth Duke of Otterburn. He'd be able to put an end to the bloodshed, the daily nightmares of the commoners. He'd be able to help heal the land and all who dwelled upon it.

And though once upon a time those ideals had meant the world to him, he could only think about his chances for keeping Curran at his side.

He started to glance toward the young man, but the hiss of steel sliding from its sheath drew his attention back to the man before him.

Gavin gazed up at him with eyes full of loving devotion. "Let me be the first to pledge to you my sword, Duke Tanis."

"Dear Gavin, I will be glad to have your counsel and your sword arm." He helped the man to his feet and embraced him. He had no other gift to give him but heartfelt thanks.

Even as Gavin clung to him, he looked around for the other man to whom he owed a great deal of gratitude. But Curran was nowhere in sight.

"We have much to talk about, your Grace," Gavin said as they parted. "Your duchy is in tatters and needs your strong hand to bring it under control."

It was true, there was much to be done. So many decisions to make. But his first decision as Duke was that he couldn't bear this burden alone. In this tempest of changes, the only thing that anchored him was Curran. He started for the door. Nothing was going to be done until he found his love and they came to an understanding.

"Tanis, where are you going?" Gavin shouted after him.

"I must find Curran."

"Curran has abandoned you already and that ring has not been on your finger long enough to warm. Despite what the two of you might have meant to each other in the past, he wants nothing to do with you now. Can you not see that?"

"No," Tanis said with conviction. Curran loved him still. He would stake his life on it.

He took the main stairs to the courtyard below, hoping he'd spot Curran along the way but he had no such luck. The only familiar face he spotted was that of Evander. "Sir Curran, where is he?"

"Gone, sir. He ordered that a horse be readied for a long ride and has already left the grounds."

Gone? Impossible!

He barely heard Evander's next words as his thoughts charged furiously after his fleeing lover.

"What of the Duke? Shall we bury his body in salted land?"

"Luthias lives, for the moment," Tanis replied. Evander's eyes widened, his mouth opened and closed in the manner of a fish. Little sound came from it so Tanis explained, "Death is his final reward. I wish to keep him from it, so that he may realize all that he has done, all that he has lost."

"But the evil inside him. It will—" Evander paused, shuddered and forced himself to continue. "More will die until the body that houses such an abomination is returned to the earth."

Tanis shook his shaggy head, understanding and even sympathizing with the common man's fear. He tried to put the servant's mind at ease. "Curran has magic the likes of which is granted only by God. He used his gift to cast the demon out and return him to the fires of hell. Now all that is left is a toothless old man with no more power than a newborn babe."

He spoke nothing less than the truth. Curran did have a magical gift, that of himself. His courage. His generous heart. And, yes, his inconvenient nobility that forced him to keep going down the roughest, solitary road long after other men would have turned toward an easier path.

"I doubt Luthias will live long, but send a trusty lad to his room thrice a day with gruel for as long as he lasts," Tanis ordered. "Fetch me upon his death and we will bury him together, you and I." He knew just the spot. A small section of the forest that reeked of rotting eggs. It was so vile a stench that even the crows and other carrion eaters avoided it.

"As you wish, sir."

Evander backed away and disappeared. Tanis left the keep, headed in the direction of the hot spring where they'd first met. He was so sure he would find Curran there, at the place that meant the most to both of them. How often had they spoken of their first time together when Curran's body was too weak to do more?

But when he reached the private glade, it was empty.

He settled on a rock, letting the memories of that night sink into his soul. Curran's eager expression, quick hands and agile body.

A body which now carried more scars than any man should have to bear.

A body, and a heart, that might be lost to him forever unless he could find the man and talk some sense into that stubborn man's head.

Overhead, Athena circled and responded with a desolate cry.

Suddenly it changed to her warning call. Tanis wiped the tears from his cheeks even as he bounded to his feet. Though they hadn't seen hide nor hair of a Celt since their withdrawal, the threat of ambush lingered until the truce could be formalized under his seal.

Tanis heard the sound of a snapping twig and spun on the balls of his feet, more than willing to fight whatever came his way.

Chapter Eighteen
~ *Loving the Man* ~

Curran stepped out from the trees. Tanis rushed him and knocked him off his feet. "You bloody bastard!" The hunt master kept him pinned to the ground by the simple act of sitting upon his chest.

Curran labored for breath under the heavy weight. "I am...sorry."

"Damn right you are, thinking a crown would patch the hole you were going to leave in my heart. You should be flogged. Beaten."

"And...perhaps...kissed?"

The weight rose, and Curran coughed air back into his lungs. Tanis pulled him to his feet, backed him into a tree and gave him the best tongue lashing a man could ask for.

No sweet seduction, this kiss. It was full of demands. Curran surrendered to each one. His questing hands sought to part fabric from skin. He hadn't done more than expose his hair-roughened chest when Tanis pulled back.

"What does this mean? Your being here?" His brown eyes were clouded with uncertainty.

Curran hated the careful way Tanis spoke. To tear off clothes and pleasure each other still came naturally to them. It was matters of the heart which caused this tension and Curran knew what he had to say wouldn't resolve it. "It means I have decided to stay and fight for your love instead of running away like a coward."

"Fight? Fight who? The siege is over."

"It is not an enemy, but rather one I have come to call a friend. It is wrong of me to bring strife into your household so soon after reclaiming the duchy, but I will fight Gavin with all but swords if I must to have your love again."

"Gavin...you think he can replace you in my heart? My love for him is a cold ember, burned out long ago. I admit I am gladdened to find his death was a ruse, but I feel no more for him than I would a brother."

"But he risked his life to give you back your land, your people, your *life*."

"So did you."

"Yes, but—"

Tanis grabbed the front of his traveling cloak and shook him hard. "Do you not understand plain English when it is spoken to you, man? I do not give one whit for the duchy. If that power will make Gavin happy, he is welcome to it. I would be quite content to spend the rest of my days as the hunt master or even a landless peasant, as long as you were with me."

"There is much that needs doing to fix this broken and abused land," Curran told him.

"Aye, and Gavin is smart enough to work it out for himself. He has no need for the likes of me to muddle in the affairs of state. A single signature will sign the whole burden over to him, and I would be glad to be rid of it."

Curran could scarcely breathe for the bands of emotion constricting his chest. This proud, strong man had surrendered so much, sacrificed so much. And now he was willing to do it again, for him. It was a gift beyond price, and Curran saw only one way to be worthy of it. It was, perhaps, the reason he had been so reluctant to leave in the first place. His future was here, with Tanis, not somewhere on the road.

"No one knows this land better than you. You should have a say in its care-taking."

Tanis' brown eyes clouded with confusion. "What are you about? I thought you wanted me to yourself."

"I want Tanis, the man, no matter what title he owns. I want your brave heart and kind soul. Give me that, and I will follow you anywhere."

"Then make haste toward my cabin. It may not be fit for man or beast after the siege, but surely there will be something to make a lover's nest, more so than the cold hard ground."

The ground would have worked just fine if Tanis had asked his opinion, but the man took off at a fast clip and Curran had to hurry to keep up with him. There was no chance to speak until they reached the little cabin in the woods. It looked like a haven of peace, as it had been for Curran time and time again.

Tanis barged through the door, then stopped in his tracks. "Well, bugger me blind and call me a beggar."

Curran couldn't keep the grin from his face as he tugged at the lacings on his boots. He freed the first one and sent it in the direction of the door. It hit the planks and slammed it closed. The second joined the first, starting a pile. He removed his belt and tossed it aside. His shirt went next, followed by his pants until he stood naked.

His lover had yet to take his eyes off the rest of the room. Not only had it escaped the wrath of the Celts, some care had been taken to keep the place tidy. It had a well-stocked pantry, and a pile of kindling in the hearth, ready to burn.

Much like the passionate fire just looking at Tanis stoked within Curran's belly. All that potential heat waited for the first spark to set it aflame.

Bewildered, Tanis said, "I don't understand. This place is not so well concealed that it would have escaped their notice. It looks as though it has been...cared for."

Curran came up behind him and wrapped his bare arms around Tanis' waist. "Gavin and I met here. When he would leave, I would sometimes stay and...see to things."

"Why?" Tanis turned in his arms. "Why did you go through the trouble?"

"It made me feel close to you in ways I could not be when we were under Luthias' mad, watchful eye." He buried his face in Tanis' neck to inhale the warm, reassuring scent of his lover. "I know it sounds foolish."

Tanis tilted his head back, forcing their gazes to meet. His dark eyes glittered, and when he spoke his voice was rough with warm emotion. "I love you, Curran Aurick."

"And I you, Tanis of Appin."

He advanced, forcing Curran to retreat. Together they tumbled onto the sleeping pallet. Curran continued to pull at Tanis' clothing until his partner's stillness caused him to look up. Tanis loomed over him. Dark and dangerous, but with a heart so pure it made Curran ache to see it there in his lover's eyes.

"What is it?" Curran asked. "Have you changed your mind?"

Tanis shook his head. "If this is a dream, I wish never to wake."

Curran's fingers found their way into the folds of leather to free Tanis' cock. "This feels like a dream to you?" he asked, stroking the hard length.

"By the Gods, yes!"

"And this?" he asked, sliding lower to take that plump head between his lips and suck until salty liquid pebbled across his tongue. "Does this feel like a dream to you?"

"Yes, damn you. Now cease this chattering before you rob me of the wits I need to answer your silly questions."

He licked the length of the hardened shaft, causing the veins within to throb with a fresh surge of blood. Tanis removed his own rags, giving Curran access to every bit of his well-muscled flesh. Curran slid under him, between his legs, where he could lick the musky scent from the huntsman's heavy sacs.

Tanis groaned and fell forward, bracing his hands against the wall. "Kill me and be done with it, man."

In answer, Curran spread Tanis' buttocks and probed that sensitive rosette with his first finger. The hunt master sucked in his breath as Curran inserted the digit up to the second knuckle. Pre-come oozed down the side of Tanis' shaft. Curran lapped it up in long strokes of his tongue, delighting in the way his lover shuddered with pleasure.

"I want to..." Tanis panted as Curran nipped at the base of his cock. "Let me..."

Curran wasn't interested in relinquishing control. It had suddenly occurred to him that Tanis always took on the position of giver during their lovemaking sessions. This time, Curran was determined that the other man learn the joys of taking instead.

He added a second finger to the first. Tanis bucked, thrusting his cock into Curran's waiting mouth. Hungrily, eagerly, Curran sucked on that stiff rod. The taste, the smell, the feel. Everything about Tanis aroused him. His own shaft filled with purpose.

Tanis rocked back and forth. Curran wiggled his fingers and the muscles constricted, driving his lover's cock past his wet, strong lips.

"Enough," Tanis ordered through lips dry from heavy panting. "Your arse is mine."

Curran permitted him to forage among the jars on the windowsill. He had plans for whatever grease the man could find. As Tanis came up with it, Curran stole it from his grasp. Beeswax.

"Good choice." Curran scooted to the end of the bed, then ordered, "On your knees."

Once in position, Tanis looked over his shoulder, his eyes clouded with doubt. "This is not what I had in mind."

"Trust me."

"With my life," Tanis replied immediately, as Curran had said to him time and time again. "But this is..."

Curran cut short the argument by spreading the viscous substance along Tanis' crack. "Trust me."

Tanis nodded, then braced himself. His fingers gripped the feather-stuffed pillow at the head of the bed. The man was so tense, penetrating him now would be like trying to push a wooden stake into frozen earth.

Without warning, Curran slapped Tanis' arse with the flat of his hand. The hunt master leaped forward and rammed his head into the wall. "What the hell was that for?" he asked, rubbing the sore spot.

"You looked as if you were expecting punishment, so I gave it to you."

"You little tease," Tanis growled, "I will give you some punishment."

Curran shook his head, his amusement fading. He wasn't going to let Tanis turn this around on him. "My way, this time," Curran reminded his lover. "Bend over."

He wasn't sure what Tanis found in his eyes, but whatever it was, it convinced him to submit. He returned to his previous position. Curran praised him with a long caress from the man's neck to his arse. "Wider," he instructed.

Tanis moved his knees further apart, giving Curran room to slide between them. He brushed his pelvis against Tanis' firm butt cheeks. His hard shaft rode up and down the crack.

"Stick me with it then," Tanis demanded.

"When I am ready." How he wanted to do just as his lover asked. To sink into that tight hole as far as he could go. To feel his balls slap against his lover's with every thrust of his hips until they both exploded. Thoughts were no longer enough but Tanis wasn't yet prepared for the next step. Sweat broke out across Curran's brow from the effort of holding back.

Soon, he promised himself. Very, very soon.

Curran prepared his cock by coating it with the beeswax. He set the jar aside and returned to the simple motion of rubbing against his lover. Like a slow, steady river, the tension flowed out of Tanis' taut arse. The familiar rhythm, even without penetration, soothed them both.

Tanis began to push back against Curran. His back arched, seeking to be filled.

That was the sign Curran had been waiting for. He ran one hand over his lover's back, then used his other to guide his hard shaft into Tanis' virgin hole. He went slowly, no more than an inch at a time. Delicious torture for both of them as Tanis stretched to accommodate him.

Finally, blessedly, Curran was buried as deep as he could go. He rested there, feeling the tight bands of muscle contract and release as they adjusted to the intrusion. Unable to remain perfectly still, his arms circled Tanis' waist and captured his fully extended cock in a firm grip. Residual wax made it easy to slide his hands over the hard length.

"Oh, bugger me," Tanis said on a sigh.

Curran chuckled. "I am."

"More," he demanded. "I want more."

Curran pulled back until the plump head was all that remained inside. Then, with a twist of his hips, he thrust in completely. His balls slapped against Tanis'. He did it again. Slow withdrawal, fast punch back in. Each time Tanis grunted long and low.

He stopped worrying and let his body take over. Short, quick strokes alternated with long, deep ones seemed to bring the maximum pleasure for both of them. As the warning tingle built up at the base of his spine, Curran leaned forward and pinched Tanis' puckered nipples. Tanis lowered his upper body until he buried his face in the pillow he still gripped between his hands.

Curran wished he could see the look on his lover's face. Next time, he vowed. Next time they would make love face-to-face. No more hiding, no more fear. He'd found his home at last.

Muscles contracted, squeezing his seed from his balls. He bucked hard, pushing so deep, pounding his flesh into Tanis as if by some miracle their two souls would become one, unbreakable whole. Under him, he could feel the huntsman's body jerk. Tanis grunted, straining to ride out his own release until the very end.

But then there was a ripping sound and...a cough?

Curran opened his eyes to see feathers floating through the air from the pillow Tanis had ripped to shreds during his powerful release. Laughter erupted from his chest as both men became covered in white plumage.

Curran lay down beside his lover. "Think this is God's way of telling us we have been bird brains?"

"I think we should take this as a sign that Fate is pleased with our decision to nest together." Tanis rolled to his side and cupped Curran's jaw. "That is what we shall do, right?"

As Curran nuzzled into his touch, he realized all his dreams had come true. His life with the Fifth Duke of Otterburn was certain to be an adventure that would require his sword...and his love. "For as long as you want me by your side, I will remain."

"Forever then." A simple, profound statement that was confirmed with a loving kiss.

Athena sent up a cry of victory as Curran and Tanis rested in each other's arms and planned their future.

About the Author

Kira Stone has been around the block...the writer's block, that is. From vamps and witches to historical heroes, from futuristic scientists to paranormal corporate executives, from Canadian werewolves to off-world shifters, Kira has written about them all. Manlove has sparked hot and heavy in many of her recent plots, but Kira also finds a lucky lady to keep the sexy heroes company from time to time. While Scotland remains her favorite place in the world, Kira is constantly in search of new adventures to add to the creative primordial ooze where her best stories are born.

To learn more about Kira Stone, please visit www.kirastonebooks.com. Send an email to Kira Stone at kirastone@gmail.com or join her Yahoo! group to join in the fun with other readers as well as Kira Stone. http://groups.yahoo.com/group/kirastonebooks

Look for these titles

Coming Soon:

One Angel's Wish

When you've lost something, it's always in the last place you look. Quinn's found Billy. Does he want to keep him?

Sex and Sexuality
© *2007 Willa Okati*

A newly-hired professor at a mountain college, Quinn is determined to put the past behind him. No more longing after men, not when he's turned his life around and even found a woman who's almost his fiancée. He's on the straight and narrow now—that is, until Billy comes along.

A force of nature, Billy sweeps Quinn off his feet and into a pair of welcoming arms. But does Quinn want to go back to being what he was, or does he dare to walk the path again after being interrupted? In the end, it's all about sex and sexuality...

Available now in ebook and print from Samhain Publishing.

Enjoy the following excerpt for *Sex and Sexuality*:

Quinn couldn't help a laugh, surprising himself by the way it pealed, loud and free, against the tiled walls of the shower. "I hope you'll like this. It's been years, though. Don't expect me to be an expert."

"I think I'm starting to get an idea of what you have in mind. Baby, there's no way to do this wrong."

"We'll see." Careful not to slip, Quinn began lowering himself onto his knees. The shower floor was cold and the tiles were hard, but he considered those to be only minor inconveniences. In his new position, Quinn was at mouth level with Billy's cock, which was growing stiffer by the second. Slowly, he reached out and took one of Billy's hips in a hand, and used the other to direct that prick to his mouth. He blew across the tip, flickering his tongue out to taste.

"Oh, God, Quinn," Billy groaned. "Please."

The thought of reducing Billy to incoherence excited Quinn. He took another deep breath, then slid his lips over the crown of Billy's cock and tried a suck. Billy groaned as Quinn applied suction, tasting the bitter saltiness of cock for what felt like the first time. Billy had his own unique flavor. Not sweet like some men Quinn had tasted once upon a time, but ashy, as if the cigarettes he constantly smoked affected every bit of his system. He found that he didn't mind the flavor. In fact, he liked it.

"Come on, come on," Billy urged, tangling his hands into Quinn's hair, growing wet with spray from the hot shower. "Fuck, Quinn. Oh, yeah."

Encouraged, Quinn slid his mouth a little further down. He was careful to keep his lips wrapped over his teeth—he remembered that much—but went slowly, not knowing how much he could take in. Billy's cock was just as large as he remembered, almost wider than his mouth could handle, but doable with a stretch.

Billy moaned, stumbling a little. Quinn registered the man pressing a hand against the wall to steady himself. He decided to help out by gripping both of Billy's hips, holding the man upright as he worked at pleasing Billy's cock. Careful not to startle Billy, he began, hesitantly, to use his tongue. Tentative laps at first, then, as he grew used to the texture, bolder strokes along the thrumming veins.

The hot water soaked Quinn as he sucked Billy's cock. Warm sheets of water coated him from hair to back, trickling around his knees. He closed his eyes and nursed at Billy's dick as if it held the milk of life. He wasn't thinking, deliberately not thinking, about anything beyond bringing Billy off. He'd stop and consider everything later, in due time.

Now was the time to use his mouth for something besides speech. Although clumsy, he lashed Billy's cock with his tongue, drawing off to probe at the slit, then sliding back down as far as he could. Suction while going down and coming up, faster and faster, until his head was bobbing and Billy was cursing a blue streak.

Billy's hands tightened in his hair. "Quinn," he choked. "Gonna—gonna—"

Quinn kneaded his hips, encouraging him without words. He wanted to taste Billy's come pouring over his tongue, to savor the flavor of the man's most intimate place. Humming under his breath, he sucked as hard as he could, and pressed hard with his tongue.

Oh! He'd forgotten. Removing one hand, Quinn brought it around to cup Billy's balls. In his eagerness, he squeezed a little too hard, rougher than most men would like.

Apparently, though, it was exactly what Billy needed. Throwing his head back and letting out a strangled roar, he came in a rush, flooding Quinn's mouth with bitter-salty come. No matter how long it had been, there were some things a man didn't forget, and Quinn swallowed the thick stuff automatically, savoring the taste as the come poured into his mouth in spurts.

He didn't stop working his tongue until Billy's orgasm had wrung itself dry, and then cleaned the man's cock off until there was no trace of semen left. Finished, he drew off and looked up, hoping for some kind of approval.

Billy was staring down at him with an unreadable look. Not even his eyes gave away what he was thinking. Quinn began to grow nervous and knew his own expression was faltering. "Didn't—didn't you enjoy...?"

"Come here," Billy growled.

GREAT
CHEAP
FUN

Discover eBooks!

THE FASTEST WAY TO GET THE HOTTEST NAMES

Get your favorite authors on your favorite reader, long before they're
out in print! Ebooks from Samhain go wherever you go, and work with
whatever you carry—Palm, PDF, Mobi, and more.

SAMHAIN
PUBLISHING, LTD

WWW.SAMHAINPUBLISHING.COM

Printed in the United States
114370LV00002B/148-153/A